FATAL FAMILY SECRETS

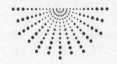

MAGGIE SHAYNE

Published by Oliver-Heber Books

0 9 8 7 6 5 4 3 2 1

❀ Created with Vellum

CHAPTER ONE

ohnny cursed *My Cousin Vinny* and slammed the steering wheel for the twelfth time. So far the steering wheel was winning.

"Maybe I should drive," Chris said. "Woman trouble?"

Johnny looked sideways at Chris, who was helping him move his stuff from his grandfather's village rental unit over the local dive bar, to Jack's cabin. "I guess not."

"Oh, man. You and Maya?"

Johnny glanced sideways, surprised. There was no him and Maya. He'd thought there might be. He'd felt as if they were maybe becoming more than friends. He was attracted to her and he was pretty sure it was mutual, and apparently the gang had picked up on that fun, flirty chemistry between them too. But things had suddenly seemed to kind of...stall. He didn't reply except to shrug.

"Dude, I'm sorry."

"Yeah. Me, too."

"You uh...want to talk about it, or...?"

Johnny shook his head. "No point." The light changed and he drove on.

"This truck is dope," Chris said in a transparent effort to change the subject. "I can't believe how quiet it is."

"It took some getting used to, it being electric."

"What did it cost, if you don't mind my asking?"

"Damned if I know. It was a gift."

Chris was waiting for further explanation. Yeah, Johnny had been pretty tight-lipped about his private life, and he knew everybody was curious. "From my wealthy, white mom and stepdad."

"Ohhhhhhh," Chris said. "So then your grandfather...?"

"My birthfather was full-blooded Iroquois, but he died when I was little. My mom remarried and I never got to know the Native side of the family. So I tracked down my grandfather last fall. Came here to get to know him, stayed with him for a month, and all of the sudden, he up and leaves without a word."

"Yeah," Chris said, nodding. "It was weird for all of us, him just leaving like he did. He's been around here forever. Longer than any of us have, I think."

"You guys were pretty close to him then?" Johnny asked.

"He didn't let too many people get close to him, especially young people. But he and Maya worked together over the years, here and there. Healing rites, house blessings, funerals, marriages. He worked with Jack sometimes too, if somebody he was reading for had a Native connection. That's how I know him, through Jack, and then he worked with us on that first case."

"The victims of the serial killer buried under Kiley's house," Johnny said, nodding.

Chris cocked a finger-gun, complete with sound effects.

"But none of you know why he left, either?"

"Nope. We figured you knew and it was none of our business."

"He said he was going to Florida to spend time with old friends and he'd be back soon."

"You have an address?"

"Yeah, I have his number, too, but he hasn't answered a call or text in a couple of days." Johnny turned a corner and drove away from the village, over a narrow, winding road with no painted lines and little intact pavement. It was pretty country, hilly and wild. "I'm getting worried, to be honest."

"You were probably hoping he'd teach you about your heritage and stuff."

"I was."

There was an extended silence and then Chris said, "People probably take one look at you and assume you're in contact with animal guides or some shit."

"That what *you* thought, Chris?"

"It's what I *hoped*," Chris said. "Is that racist? I hope it's not racist. I'm black and gay, I know better." He shook his head like he regretted his words, but then smiled at him and added, "But you have to admit, it would've been cool."

Johnny attempted to give him a stern glare, but he couldn't keep the laugh inside. Chris elbowed him in the ribs and started laughing, too, and then a person ran in front of the truck and THUD. He felt the impact, slammed the brakes, and saw the person lurch and tumble toward the ditch, all in the space of a second.

They both dove out of the truck, which had skidded sideways in the road, and ran toward the shoulder. Johnny's heart was in his throat. In the ditch, a skinny teenager pushed his long, dark bangs off his face. His eyes were brown. There was dirt smeared on his forehead.

"Are you okay?"

"Are you hurt?" they asked at the same time, and Johnny reached out to clasp the kid's hand and help him up.

"I'm okay," he said. "I think." He brushed at his clothes and stepped out of the ditch onto the shoulder of the country road, looking around them as if he expected to see someone else.

Johnny looked around, too. The paved part of the road had ended half a mile back. This part was dirt and gravel. Every spring the town road crews dumped fresh gravel on top, and every fall it was mostly all ground in or gathered along the shoulders as a blatant challenge to joggers and cyclists.

The kid had come tearing out of the woods off to the left. The right side of the road was a wide patch of dead looking meadow that Chris said would be thick with grass and wildflowers once spring took hold. As of now they were stuck in the in-between. Snow melting. Temps warming. Mud everywhere.

"I'm sorry, man," Johnny said. "I didn't see you."

"It was my fault. I ran out in front of you." The kid turned to glance behind him.

"Why do I get the feeling somebody was chasing you?" Chris asked, following the kid's gaze and taking the same visual tour Johnny just had, but from the perspective of someone who knew the area better than he did.

"You *see* anybody chasing me?"

"Ah, the sarcasm of sixteen," Chris said, from the ripe old age of twenty-three.

"Seventeen," the kid said.

Chris shrugged. "So why were you running, then?"

"You ever hear of cross-country?"

Chris looked at Johnny. Johnny looked at the kid's shoes - basketball shoes. He wore them with jeans and a winter coat. Not exactly running gear.

"Isn't the high school just the other side of that woodlot?" Chris asked. "That where you're coming from?"

"Yeah, and I have to get back." He started to turn away, but Johnny felt an irresistible urge not to let him leave just yet. Something was wrong.

"Don't run off. Come on, school's out by now anyway, isn't it? My pal Chris just has a curious mind. I'm Johnny."

"Ryan." He pushed his hair again. He had one of those long side bangs that guys his age were constantly pushing out of their eyes.

"Can we give you a ride somewhere, Ryan?" Johnny nodded at the truck, sitting cockeyed in the road.

"Looks like you're already on your way to somewhere." Ryan said, eyeing the load of furniture and boxes in the pickup's bed.

"I'm moving into my new place," Johnny said. It was odd how it felt like a lie to call it his place. It was Jack's place, but Jack was currently co-habiting with Kiley over at Spook Central, so Johnny had agreed to rent his log cabin. "It's only about a mile from here, actually."

Ryan nodded slowly, then said, "I'll take a ride, yeah, but I'll help you unload first. If you want."

"Shoot, are you sure you weren't dropped in front of us by the Moving Fairy?" Chris asked, grinning ear to ear. "Hop in."

Ryan hopped in, taking the truck's back seat. As he pulled into motion, Johnny saw the kid looking behind them. He glanced sideways and saw Chris noticing it, too. No way somebody wasn't chasing him. Johnny felt heat rising up the back of his neck. He knew about bullies. He'd dealt with his share of them, having been the only native in his mostly white private school.

Somebody was bullying Ryan. Johnny decided on the spot that he was going to find a way to help.

He looked across at Chris, who met his eyes and gave a single, firm nod, as if he knew what Johnny was thinking and was in full agreement.

Kiley stood on the front porch of her gorgeous, hundred-and-thirty-year-old Victorian house, wielding a long-handled paint roller back and forth over the porch ceiling. She wished Jack was doing it, but he seemed to think the Magic Shop ought to be open every once in a while, so he was there.

The entire house needed painting. All of it, from the witch's hat turrets to the sunburst high peak panels to the turned posts and spindles. All of that was on the schedule for *actual* spring, not this crazy, windy, precursor known as March. But the porch, Maya had insisted, could not wait.

Because ghosts.

Maya was manning another long-handled roller a few feet away. She said, "Careful not to let it–" just as a glob of paint dropped right onto Kiley's upturned face, splatting across her nose. "–drip on your head," Maya finished.

Kiley lowered her roller to the nearby tray, leaned the handle against the wall, and pulled a ratty old dish towel from her farmer jeans' back pocket to wipe the pale blue-going-on-gray paint away.

"I'd think you were pulling a Tom Sawyer trick on me, if it wasn't my own house we were painting."

"Oh, it's a trick, all right," Maya said. "Just not on you."

"I get the silver coins and old iron nails hidden near every door and window, since you say ghosts allegedly hate silver and iron."

"That's the lore."

"And I get the bottle tree..." Kiley trailed off, because the breeze came up almost as if in response to her thoughts, and the bottles of every shape, size and color dangling from the big elm tree began to clink and clatter. The sound was magical. "I kind of love the bottle tree."

"I love it, too. It's supposed to trap and confuse malevolent spirits," Maya said. "I figured we'd try everything." She finished the final stroke and lowered her roller into an empty bucket.

"Including this pale blue paint on the porch floor and ceiling," Kiley said. "Which I still do not understand."

"Not just blue. *Haint* Blue."

"Haint Blue?" Kiley arched one eyebrow. "The hell it haint." Then she slapped her thigh and laughed at her own joke.

Maya laughed, but not enough. "The lore says ghosts can't

cross water. Haint Blue is supposed to look like water so they don't come in."

Kiley looked up at the porch ceiling. Then she looked at Maya again. "I have never seen water that color."

"The circle I cast will be the part that counts," Maya said, choosing to ignore her keen observation. "I'll place wards at the four directions and ask our local elementals to keep watch."

"Elementals."

"Nature spirits." She looked around the back yard and smiled as if some old friend was looking back at her. Then she returned her gaze to Kiley and apparently read her skeptical face. "Be doubtful all you want. When I finish, not one ghost is ever going to set foot in your house again."

Someone laughed from inside. A female someone. Kiley frowned and looked at the closed door. "Who *was* that? Is the TV on?"

"Who was what?" Maya asked. She unscrewed the extra-long handle from the paint roller and picked up the bucket with the used rollers inside.

Kiley grabbed the paint and the tray and the rest, and they carried the mess around to the side of the house where there was an outside spigot. The ground was still cold and hard, but would soften to sticky later in the day. Most of the snow had melted except for a patch here and there and the powdered sugar dusting from the night before.

Maya picked up a roller and began rinsing the Haint Blue away under the faucet, over a bucket.

"So, what's up with you and Johnny?" Kiley asked. She'd been dying to ask, and now she was asking. For a while there, it had seemed like they were ... not together, but maybe pre-together. But the past couple of days, things between them had seemed colder than the water coming out of that spigot.

Maya didn't look up from her task, her hands apparently immune to the chill. "Nothing's up with me and Johnny."

"Why not? It seemed like something was kind of brewing there, you'll pardon the witch pun."

Maya smiled at the pun, finished rinsing her roller and tray, and made way for Kiley, who began rinsing her own. She said, "So here's the thing."

Inside her head, Kiley pulled up a chair and a bowl of popcorn.

"He was talking about hunting. How torn he feels about it, because he knows it's part of his heritage and the way his ancestors survived, and yet he doesn't think he could do it himself."

"So, you're breaking up with him because you don't eat meat and he's of two minds about hunting?" Kiley stopped herself from blurting how unlike Maya that seemed.

"Not breaking up. There's nothing to break up."

There was something, though. Kiley had seen it. Everyone had. The two seemed as drawn to each other as bees to flowers. "Maybe he just wanted your opinion as a vegan?"

And since when, Kiley wondered, had she become such a Johnny-Maya fan? Didn't matter, she was. They just felt right together, ages be damned.

"No. It wasn't that," Maya said. "Actually, looking back, I think he wanted my opinion on all of it. But you know, it was the perfect opening, so I had to reply, "Imagine you're a deer." Only she pronounced it "dee-yuh" in perfect Marisa Tomei. "You're prancin' along, you get thirsty, you spot a little brook, and you put your little deer-lips down to the cool, clear water... BAM! A fuckin' bullet rips off part of your head!"

By the time she finished, Kiley was laughing so hard she'd splashed paint-tinted water on her bibs. "That was dead on."

"Yeah," Maya said. "Only he didn't get the reference."

Kiley turned off the spigot, her brain trying to catch up. "Well, not everybody's seen *My Cousin Vinny*."

"He didn't get the reference because he wasn't born yet."

"Oh." Kiley frowned. "Ouch. Okay. But gee... of all people, I wouldn't have expected you to be worried about an age difference."

"An eighteen-*year* age difference."

"Nineteen." Kiley bit her lip too late to keep the comment from spilling out, and fully deserved the fake death glare Maya sent her.

"You've been doing the math in your head. Everyone probably has," Maya said. "Doesn't matter. It's too wide a gap."

"So…you broke up with him?"

"We were never even dating. I mean, I think that's where he wanted to take things, and maybe I did too, but that felt like the Universe asking me what the hell I think I'm doing." She shook her head. "It wouldn't be fair to him." She turned a little, so her face was averted. "And anyway, I don't want to talk about it. I'm trying to make sense of it in my own head, you know?"

"And it's none of my business." Kiley shrugged and shut off the spigot. "I don't know why, but it feels like it is."

Maya faced her again, her friendly smile back in place, but it wasn't hiding her sadness at all. "Well, unless you want me asking you what Jack likes in bed, knock it off."

"Reverse cowgirl." Kiley picked up the pail full of freshly washed rollers, turned and pointed, "But not until near the end, because it tends to speed things up." She made fireworks of her fingers and said, "Boom."

"OmyGod, please stop." Maya held up both hands, but she laughed anyway.

Kiley winked and felt warm and mushy about the friendship blooming between the two of them. It was fun, sassy, teasing, and sincere. She opened the hatchway to carry the tools down to the basement, but only went as far as the bottom of the stairs, set the bucket there, and leaned the long roller handles against the concrete wall. She gave a quick look deeper into the basement. The insurance had paid for the dungeon room underneath it to be filled in, and fresh new concrete poured on the basement floor. Everything was clean and new down there. But still...

She backed up the stairs and closed the hatch.

"Still creeps you out, doesn't it?"

"Yeah. Jack wants to finish it and light up the space. Make it a game room or something. But I'll never feel comfortable no matter what he does."

"I don't know if I would, either. A lot of women died down there." Maya took a breath, but then nodded and said, "But we helped them find peace and cross over. We did that."

"And in the process, we made this place the most popular way station between heaven and hell." Kiley rubbed her hands down the backs of her jeans as the two of them walked around front to head inside. "Yes, indeed, Maya, I really love that bottle tree," she said, when a breeze caused the bottles to jingle and clink again, just before she closed the front door.

"Johnny loves it, too," Maya said.

Kiley looked over her shoulder. "Oh, he does?" she asked. "What does Chris think of it?"

"I don't know," Maya said. They were standing in the little foyer, heeling off their shoes.

Kiley said, "I don't know either. But I know what Jack thinks of it."

"What does Jack think of it?" Maya was clearly puzzled by the discussion.

"He thinks if the wind blows too hard, the bottles will break, and it'll be a lot of work cleaning up every little bit of glass from the lawn. But you asked the wrong question."

Maya blinked at her, deliberately not asking what the right question would be, but Kiley wasn't going to let a little thing like that stop her when she was on a roll.

"The question you should've asked is, *why* do I know what Jack thinks of it? And the answer is, for the same reason you know what Johnny thinks of it. You're tuned in to him. And I'm just saying, he's an amazing guy."

Maya blinked and averted her face. Were her eyes welling up? "Most amazing guy I know." And then she rubbed her arms like she was cold.

Kiley went into the living room and had the remote in her hand before she noticed the black TV screen. "The TV isn't on. Then what *did* I hear before?"

"Well, what did you think you heard?" Maya asked, pulling on a long knit sweater. It was sage green and set off her long blond hair to perfection, Kiley thought.

"I thought...it sounded like a woman laughing."

Maya frowned at her, then got that focused look of someone listening hard.

Kiley looked out the window and saw a group of middle school kids walking a dozen yards away on the opposite side of the road. Maybe not the first group to pass by. Maybe she'd just heard some kids walking home from school. Maybe when she could afford to paint more than just the porch, they wouldn't give the place such a wide berth.

No, they still would. The cops had been digging up bodies not that long ago, after all. Hell, if she didn't own it, she'd probably give the place a wide berth herself.

"You don't think it was another...?" Maya let her voice trail off, her meaning clear.

"A *ghost*? No way. I don't hear ghosts. I'm a muggle. You, Jack and Johnny are the woo-woo crew."

"Woo-woo crew, huh?" Maya asked. "I like it. We should have t-shirts made. Spook Central Woo-Woo Crew."

Kiley rolled her eyes, glanced at the street again, and hoped to God one of those kids or their cohorts had a laugh that sounded like a middled-aged chain smoker with a whiskey chaser. But she doubted it.

CHAPTER TWO

Chris and Ryan not only unloaded Johnny's worldly possessions, but helped him arrange things around the place, too.

Jack had left behind most of the furniture. The living room set was decent. The brown sofa was the softest thing he'd ever laid on. There was also a green chair and a wooden coffee table. The kitchen appliances were all black, and he liked that way better than stainless, not that he was fussy. He'd brought his own bed and dresser, which he'd bought for his grandfather's apartment when the old man had told him he could stay. And he'd done it with his own money, not the account his parents had set up, and which they funded. He'd use it, in a pinch, but he'd been donating most of it now that he was making a modest living helping people with ghost problems.

Everybody else in the gang had other jobs. Jack owned the Magic Shop, a tourist-favorite in the village, and Chris worked for him there. Kiley wrote for the Burnt Hills Gazette, and Maya was… well Maya. She raked it in as a celebrity witch on the internet. Books, blogs, interviews, etc. She tried to play it down, didn't seem comfortable with her own popularity. She'd told him once she could only do it because she was mostly behind a computer screen, safely ensconced in her own space.

Johnny had still not heard back from his grandfather, but it wasn't the first time John Redhawk, the elder, had taken off on a radio-silent retreat. He was usually back the next day, though.

Once they had everything unloaded and boxes and things sorted into the rooms where they belonged, they all sat on the sofa, the three of them, and cracked two beers and a root beer. The kid took the root beer and said, "Full disclosure. I'm not twenty-one til June of three years from now."

"Yeah, I don't see any cops," Chris said as if the root beer were the real deal.

"Are we gonna be in trouble with your parents or anything?" Johnny asked, no longer referring to the beverage.

"Probably." The kid looked around and it actually made Johnny feel nervous. He looked around, too.

"So...now that we've bonded over physical labor," Chris said, "You wanna tell us who you were running from back there?"

Ryan shook his head. "Humiliation?" He took a long sip from his bottle. "I was with a girl, and ... I guess we got caught."

"Got caught?"

"Parents, you know." He tipped the root beer up and downed most of it, then burped.

"Parents," Johnny said, deadpan. "How old was this girl?"

"Not *her* parents."

"Yours?"

Ryan nodded.

"So, three months from eighteen, and your parents are following you around trying to keep you from having sex?" Chris looked at Johnny, frowning. "That's rough, man."

Ryan set the empty bottle on the floor and said, "I gotta go," rising up and taking three long strides toward the door.

"Thought you needed a ride."

"I can walk."

He opened the door just as a little white EV skidded to a stop in the driveway. An angry female got out and came striding right up to the kid. "What the actual hell, Ryan?"

"Jeeze, Breia, it's fine. I'm fine."

"What is this, huh?" She pushed past him right into the living room. Johnny rose automatically and Chris did, too. God, she was furious. "You feeding beer to a teenager? You want to go to prison, or should I just kick your asses myself?" She was all of five feet even, but Johnny bet she would try anyway.

"He said he'd be twenty-one in June," Chris said, grinning at Ryan like it was an inside joke.

"He had root beer," Johnny said, shooting Chris a look. He pointed to the empty bottle on the floor near the couch.

The angry woman was still standing in the doorway, one hand holding the screen door open because she hadn't come all the way inside. She saw the bottle and seemed to calm down. "Sorry. I get so damn worried when I can't *find* him." She emphasized the word find with a look at the kid. They looked alike, Johnny noticed. Same smooth dark hair, same skin tone, same brown eyes.

The screen door slammed open, ripping itself from her hand and hitting the wall behind it. She yipped and pulled her hand to her chest, palm up.

Johnny crossed the room fast, grabbed the screen and pulled it closed. No resistance. Wind must have caught it and yanked it right out of her hand.

He looked at her upturned palm. The finger pads were scraped and red.

"Can I just...is there a bathroom?"

"Yeah, through there." Johnny pointed and she went in and closed the door while he tried to remember if he'd put a roll of TP out yet.

Chris said, "You're in deep shit with your mom."

Ryan went, "Shyeah. *Mom.*" He pushed his dark hair off his

forehead, glancing a little nervously toward the now closed door. "Breia's my sister."

She came out of the bathroom, holding her hands up in front of her like a surgeon.

"Ah, crap, no towels are unpacked yet," Johnny said. "I'm sorry. I'm just moving in. Let me—" He stammered more words as he searched boxes for a towel, thought he'd found one, pulled it out and offered it to her.

The kid burst out laughing, and he could tell Breia was trying really hard not to grin. "That's okay," she said, and wiped her hands on her purple leggings.

He looked down and saw he was holding a pair of his jockey shorts. Biker style. "Shit." He shoved them into the nearest box.

"I'm Breia," she said at last. "Ryan is my brother."

"I'm Johnny. This is Chris."

Chris gave an awkward wave. "We ran into Ryan on the road," Chris said. "Offered him a ride. He said he'd help us unload as payback."

"Well, now he has a ride. Come on, Ryan."

"Stop telling me what to do."

"It's my job to tell you what to do."

"No, it's not. It was our parents' job, and they've been dead since I was a baby. They don't get to run my life and neither do you. I do."

Chris said, "Dead? But then who–"

Johnny kicked him in the shin, because no way was he going to let him tell Ryan's sister he'd been caught making it with a girl. Or trying to.

She didn't notice it, distracted by her brother, who was reaching for the beer Chris had left on the mantle like he was going to down it right in front of her. It flew off just as he made contact with the bottle, hit the floor, and didn't break. It just spun, spilling beer. Johnny felt like he'd blinked and missed something as he put his foot on the bottle to stop its spinning.

"I didn't do that. That wasn't me!" The kid closed his eyes and clenched his jaw. When he opened them again, he said, "Sorry. I didn't mean it."

Johnny picked up the bottle. "It's the ceremonial spilling of the first beer," he said. "My new place is now official, and you got the honor, kid."

"I think that makes you part of the gang now," Chris said. Johnny thought he was enjoying having someone younger than him around.

Ryan was no longer defiant. He looked a little shaken. "How did you find me, anyway?" He asked his sister.

"If I tell you, how will I find you next time?"

"You tracked my phone," he accused. "Jeeze." He turned toward the door.

"Wait, Ryan. Here." Johnny pulled a twenty from the clip in his pocket and handed it to the kid. "For all the help."

Ryan took the bill and shoved it into his jeans' pocket.

His sister caught his eye and turned her glare up to high-beam, so he said, "Thanks for the ride and the root beer and everything." Then he headed out to the waiting car.

Johnny stood there, face to face with Breia. She smiled awkwardly. He said, "I'm sorry about your parents," because he couldn't think of anything else. "I should've made him call you as soon as we got here. Maybe we shouldn't have offered him a ride at all. It just seemed like the thing to do at the time."

"No, it's not your fault." She stood a few feet from him, looking him right in the eyes. "You didn't do anything wrong."

She was *really* pretty. But he wanted Maya.

But Maya had cooled toward him, maybe over *My Cousin Vinny*.

Chris cleared his throat, snapping him out of his thoughts. He sent Johnny a "what the hell, you're single" look, and said, "I'm gonna go exchange contact info with Ryan." Then he went out the door.

Johnny told himself to ask her out. She was looking at him like the answer would be yes if he did. But no. No, it was way too soon, and he hadn't given up. "It was really good to meet you, Breia."

She reached across the space between them, and clasped his hands in hers. They were warm and soft and very small, and she had neat, pretty nails. "It was nice to meet you, too." She let his hands go and turned toward the door.

He walked out with her onto the porch. Chris was leaning on the car, talking to Ryan, who sat inside, mostly listening.

"Is your brother okay, do you think?"

She looked over at him. He had his hands in his pockets. She said, "I don't know. I don't think so."

"I feel like I should tell you... We were driving along, and he came tearing out of the woods right into our path. I was driving. I hit him. Not hard, I mean, we weren't moving very fast. It's a back road, but it knocked him back a few feet. You should have him looked at."

"I will."

"And send me the bill. I'll take care of it."

He looked at her. He'd been trying not to, because she was really beautiful. Big brown eyes and dark brown hair in a short, fun style. Just then, she looked pained. "But...why was he running?"

"I don't know, he said his parents caught him with a girl. But clearly that's not it."

She nodded. "Thank you for telling me."

"I wouldn't have, but I...I have a feeling he's in trouble. Somehow."

"Yeah, I have the same feeling," she said. "I've had it for a while, to be honest."

He could tell by looking at her that something was weighing her down, and kind of dimming her light. She looked tired.

"If he needs friends, we're here for that. Chris is only a few years older and they hit it off big time. Spent twenty minutes talking about computer games in what sounded like their own language."

"Thanks. That's sweet."

"That goes for you, too, okay? If there's anything we can do, let us know."

"I will," she said, and she spent an extra few seconds gazing at his face, maybe waiting for him to say more, or maybe thinking about saying something more herself. But in the end, she did neither, just smiled her sweet smile, and turned away. He didn't walk her to the car.

CHAPTER THREE

*K*iley held up a hand for silence, because the doorbell, just installed that morning, had just chimed the familiar pipe organ chords of *Toccata and Fugue in D Minor*.

It was the programmable electronic bell's maiden voyage with an actual visitor, and it was kind of cool that everyone was still there for it, gathered around pizza in the living room, chatting about the raft of clients they'd had in the new year.

The cops had held a presser just before Christmas to announce they'd solved the fifteen-year-old murder of Gabriel York. On an anonymous tip—from Kiley—a reporter–a friend of Kiley's—had asked, on-camera, about the rumor that local ghost-busting company, Spook Central, had been instrumental in solving the cold case.

It didn't matter that Lieutenant Mendosa had skillfully dodged the question by talking about the many officers and resources, including community members, who had contributed to bringing justice to bear, yada, yada, yada.

Spook Central was a catchy name and it had caught. They were about as busy as they could comfortably be, with Jack still running his new age shop in the touristy part of the village, and Kiley still writing pieces for the Burnt Hills Gazette. Maya was doing all her influencer stuff—which was a lot. Kiley had started following her. There were blog posts and video messages and books. Maya, it turned out, was kind of a big deal. Chris had his job with Jack, and she didn't know what the hell Johnny did.

The doorbell played its horror movie riff again.

Kiley tipped her head sideways and wrinkled her nose at Jack. "I still think that song's awfully dire. Wasn't that in *Phantom of the Opera* or something?"

"*Dracula*, maybe?" Jack asked.

"Not, *Dracula*, but lots of others, starting with *Dr. Jekyl and Mr. Hyde* in 1932," Chris said. The song had been his suggestion. "Even before that, orchestras performed it live for silent films in the genre so frequently some complained it was over-used."

"Wow," she replied. "That's a long and noble history."

Missing her sarcasm entirely, Chris replied, "That's why it's the perfect doorbell chime for Spook Central." He looked at the others "What's everyone else think?"

"I wanted the wind chime effect instead of music," Maya said.

"Yeah, but that's too–" Kiley wiggled her fingers in the air trying to think of a term that wouldn't offend her. "–too the opposite of dire."

"You were going to say airy fairy," Maya accused. "I heard you thinking it."

"You heard yourself *thinking* I thought it." Kiley had totally been thinking it.

"That was brilliant. You are brilliant," Jack praised, then nodded at Maya as if daring her to out logic his girlfriend.

"I still say the rif from *Enter Sandman. Dun duh DA DA dun.*" Johnny strummed an air-guitar. Maya laughed, and he looked her way, and then they both stopped smiling and looked away from each other.

Kiley filed the exchange away in her mind. Maya claimed

nothing had ever happened between them. Then why did her eyes look so full of longing when she looked his way?

The doorbell chimed again.

Kiley nodded. "Yeah, way too dire."

"Guys," Chris said, "I think we have an actual visitor."

Kiley realized there was someone at the door, and then said, "It better be. *Actual*, that is." She headed across the huge living room toward the mini-foyer and oversized front door. The door-bell system had been a contribution from Maya. Its speaker was hidden behind the original doorbell chime cover. You could program in pretty much any sound you wanted, including a werewolf howl, which had already been tried and ruled out, thank you Jack.

She loved the thing.

She heard a voice saying, "I knew this was a mistake," and opened the door just as a woman was starting to turn away. She turned back.

"Sorry about the wait," Kiley said. "We were..." She stopped there, because the woman was looking past her at someone behind her and reacting. Her brown eyes widened a little, and she pushed her dark hair behind one ear. "You," she said, lowering her gaze.

Kiley looked over her shoulder. Johnny stood there, hands in his pockets. And behind him, Maya was looking on with a curi-ously resigned smile.

"Oh, um, hi, Breia, I uh–" Johnny shrugged and glanced behind him toward Maya, who quickly looked away and tried to pretend she hadn't noticed a thing.

Kiley was beyond riveted, and kept elbowing Jack to make sure he wasn't missing out. He kept looking at her, and then looking where she was looking, and then at her again, with an "I don't know what you want me to see" expression. His adorable eyebrows kind of quirked up and she wanted to kiss him. God, she made herself sick.

Chris came jogging to the door and to the rescue. "Hey, girl! Everybody, this is Breia. We met her and her brother Ryan today out by Jack's cabin. Well, Johnny's cabin, that is. Come on in, Breia. How did you track us down here, anyway?"

She entered and Jack closed the door behind her.

"I didn't," she said. "Um, track you guys down, I mean. I didn't know you worked here. I came here because... I think my brother is being haunted."

"Oh!" Johnny said, in a voice that came out silly high. He cleared his throat and said, "In that case..."

"Follow me," Kiley said," but before she could take a step, the doorbell chimed, only this time, it was in a whole new cadence. And then it repeated.

"Is that..."

"It is," Maya said, and then she sang, "It begins to tell, 'round midnight, 'round midnight."

"It's kind of perfect," Jack said. Makes you want to..." He swept Kiley into an exaggerated waltz step, with a dip at the end, and she laughed out loud.

Then he stood her up again, and she smoothed her blouse, her cheeks all red for some asinine reason. Maya was smiling at her the way you smile at cute puppies or ugly children.

She wiped the bliss off her face and reminded herself of the foremost question. "Who added that to the doorbell program?"

Everybody looked at everybody else, but nobody took credit.

Kiley opened the door. It was just a package from the 'Zon. She brought it in and led the way into the library that they'd turned into Spook Central Headquarters. It had its own entrance, but there was still work to be done outside. Now that spring was at hand, the flagstone path out there would get some much-needed attention and their very cool sign would be mounted on a pole. Come to think of it, they'd need to link Maya's doorbell system to the office entrance, too.

The library was the largest room in the house, and its

makeover had been a collaboration. Kiley had wanted the neat little sitting area for interviewing clients to match the style of the place, Victorian. Jack had wanted the coffee niche and a mini fridge for snacks. Chris had set up the computer bar along the back wall, a counter with three tall stools, currently hosting three large monitors. The gigantic painting, Dogs Playing Poker, was also Chris's gift. Kiley hated the thing but had to let it stay because Democracy. They had not purchased any of this stuff; Chris had brought it from his apartment.

Yes, he was *that* big a nerd. Thank God.

The floor-to-ceiling bookshelves on two and a half walls were slowly filling up. Very slowly. Chris bought a couple of volumes out of every paycheck and brought them in. Jack had brought in a copy of every title the magic shop carried, too. And Maya had stored volumes there for easy access; ancient-looking tomes, a stack of beautifully bound journals, their pages filled with hand-writing, and stacks of three-ring binders bulging with printed pages on heavy vellum-like paper.

The bookshelves still had a lot of bare space, though. They'd placed some crystals and curios and a couple of plants in the empty spots. Some were Maya's own and others had come from Jack's shop. They definitely needed more stuff, but Kiley supposed things would accumulate over time.

She had framed the front-page story about Gabriel York's body being found, and hung it on a big, empty section of the wall that was reserved for their cases. The only other story there was the best one about the discovery of the bodies in the basement, the case that had brought them together. So far, those were the only two of their cases that had made the papers. Most of them didn't even have real ghosts, and their task was mainly to put the clients' minds at ease.

Kiley watched Breia taking it all in while Jack was saying, "Have a seat. Can we get you something to drink? Coffee, tea, water?"

"No, thank you." Breia slid into an overstuffed chair. It was a replica Victorian, all the scrollwork and wood trim of the real thing, but way more comfortable. There was one other chair and a love seat, all the same style and dark burgundy shade. Floral throw pillows were as busy as Kiley had been willing to go, even though Maya said the furniture cried out for it. A fake Oriental rug in the same shades lay atop the hardwood.

Kiley took the love seat, Jack sat beside her, and slid his hand over hers, making her look into his eyes for a second. If felt good to her toes, that little intimate exchange, just between the two of them.

Chris took the other chair. Johnny stood near one of the bookshelves, kind of leaning on it with an elbow.

Maya went to the computer bar on the other side of the room, slid up onto a stool and started tapping keys. "I'll start a client file," she said. "Can I get the spelling on that name?"

"Breia Sousa." Breia spelled her name as Maya keyed it in. "And my brother is Ryan."

"What makes you think he's being haunted?" Kiley asked.

"I didn't, at first. I thought he was just acting out. His girl-friend dumped him at the winter formal last week. And then I don't know what happened, but I know for sure it's not what they said happened." She looked right at Johnny when she said that, and their eyes locked, and Kiley slanted a quick look at Maya to see if she noticed, but she had her eyes on the monitor in front of her. She glanced back at Johnny, but he wasn't there.

Johnny fell into Breia's story. Actually, it felt more like he was being sucked into it. One minute he was standing there, listening, closing his eyes to concentrate instead of worrying about another unanswered call to his grandfather, and the next he was standing in a dark room full of dancing teenagers. There were sparkles on the walls and the hardwood floor was painted for basketball. He was at a high school dance. A mirrored ball spun from the ceiling and streamers did their best to disguise the upraised basketball nets.

He looked around and spotted Ryan and a girl who had purple streaks in her blond hair. They were having an animated discussion. He looked upset.

Johnny headed toward them, raising a hand and yelling, "Hey, Ryan!"

Ryan looked at Johnny like he didn't know him. And then he had one of the chaperones or a teacher or a dad up in his face, saying, "I'm sorry, I'm not sure you're supposed to be here. Can I help you find someone, or...?"

Leaning sideways, Johnny tried to see past the guy.

"I'm really sorry, Ryan," the girl said. "But I'm with Jimmy now. Accept it." She turned and strode away, and every time her high heel hit the gym floor, Johnny felt it like a knife in Ryan's heart. It was so real, he put a hand on his own chest.

That was when it hit him that he was in the past. He grabbed hold of his own forearm, then poked the chaperone, who was side-stepping to block his progress. Solid. Real.

He felt dizzy and disoriented, and a little flutter of panic wondered how he was going to get back where he belonged again. Or if he even could. But then he found an opening and dodged around the chaperone guy.

The girl stomped away and Ryan stomped after her and Johnny got nervous. "Just let her go, dude!"

Ryan either didn't hear him or didn't listen. He caught up to the girl right in front of the refreshment table. Then he reached out and flipped the punchbowl right onto her. *Right* onto her. The entire right side of her white dress was dripping with red and she started screaming. It was a scene right out of Carrie. The music stopped, and the lights came up, and somebody thought it was blood and screamed, and a riot was about to break out.

And then Johnny held up both hands and said, "Wait, wait, wait, hold up a sec!" And everything froze.

He looked around, blinking. Okay, that was weird. He could move among the kids, around them, but none of them moved. Some of the punch droplets were still airborne, frozen there. He frowned and looked at his hands, the way he was holding them up in a universal message to stop.

"Go back." He said it quietly and moved his hands like wiping rain off a window, right to left, and the whole freaking place rewound like an old VHS movie. He lowered his hand and everything came back to normal. Johnny focused exclusively on Ryan's left hand as he pursued the girl, caught up to her, and reached out for her.

Then he held up his hand. "Stop!"

Everything froze.

"This is freaking cool." But that wasn't the point just then. He watched closely. Ryan's hand was inches from the girl's arm and in front of the punch bowl, which was already in the process of flipping. The first splash hadn't even reached its target yet.

Johnny moved his focus to Ryan's face. He was looking left, horrified. So, Johnny looked there, too. And then he narrowed his eyes and looked closer, because there was something behind the punch bowl, behind the refreshment table. Just a spot in the air where it rippled, like heat waves rising from hot pavement.

What *was* that?

CHAPTER FOUR

"*J*ohnny!"

There was a weird, full-body impact when Johnny snapped back into his own time. He almost lost his balance and found himself staring into Maya's blue eyes as she braced him with her hands on his shoulders. A long, yellow bang fell across one of them. He almost brushed it behind her ear, stopped himself after the barest movement. She dropped her hands and looked away.

Everyone was staring at him, asking with their eyes *What the hell was that?*

"I'm okay, I'm okay. Please, finish your story."

"Johnny, you just like…disappeared for a second," Maya said.

"I did?"

"You all saw it." Maya looked around, and so did Kiley.

"I didn't see it," Kiley said. "Not…really."

Nobody else looked as if they had, either, and then Jack said, "I saw it. It was like you flickered. You blinked out and back on. It was—"

"So fast," Maya said.

Jack looked her way and nodded.

"Trick of the light?" Johnny asked, nodding toward the window, and then with a little bit of a scowl, toward Breia. As in *not in front of the client, okay?* "Go ahead, please finish your story."

"I already did. Ryan was suspended for that," Breia said. "Three days. And he just kept saying it wasn't him, that he didn't do it."

Johnny moved closer to where Breia sat. His knees were a slightly unsteady, and he felt sick to his stomach. Not to mention that his mind was churning with ways to explain what had just happened to him.

Jack and Maya said he'd vanished and reappeared, adding to his certainty that he had actually, physically, time-traveled.

Maya stayed where she was, where he'd been a moment ago, near the fireplace, but her eyes were on him.

"There have been other incidents," Breia said. "Things keep happening to people who've crossed Ryan in some way. And the worst was that night when you met him. A kid fouled him on the basketball court. He was guarding him tight. He and Ryan got tangled up and hit the floor. The other kid's leg was so badly broken that the bones were sticking out."

Kiley sucked air through her teeth and shot Jack a look.

Chris said, "It's not basketball season."

"It's a spring league," Briea said, clearly puzzled that was what he'd taken from her tale. "Ryan ran off the court, grabbed his clothes from the locker room and left the building. Somebody saw him head into the woods getting dressed as he went."

"No wonder he was running like he was," Chris said. "He knew he'd be blamed. Again."

"I was driving around looking for him when I tracked his phone to your place."

Johnny nodded and said, "What happened today, Breia? Something brought you here."

"The coach called. Ryan's off the team for the rest of the

season. He got really upset when I told him, slammed into his room, and I heard him in there yelling."

"What did he say?" Johnny asked it softly, and when she met his eyes, she held onto his gaze as if it were a life preserver.

She took a breath and repeated her brother's words. "'Why don't you just die, you motherfucking ghosts.'" She closed her eyes. "And for the first time, I thought about it. Things he's said, or started to say. The way he's been acting, his anxiety and insomnia. It would explain everything."

"Everything?" Kiley asked. "Have there been other incidents?"

Breia opened her bag, pulled out a file folder, and handed it over. "I've kept notes. I was thinking he might be having mental health issues and his doctor would want to know, but now..."

"So, you want us to find out for sure," Jack said.

"I aleady know for sure. He didn't do it. I'd like you to find proof." She looked at each of them in turn. "I told the coach he didn't do it. He said he'd give me a week to prove it." She shrugged her shoulders and pushed her short, dark hair up higher on her head. "So, prove it."

The gang all looked at each other. Jack said, "I don't know if we can."

Kiley sprang off the loveseat like a jack-in-the-box. "If we can't, then who can?" she asked. "Don't we at least have to try? It's a kid, for crying out loud."

Breia sent Johnny a wide-eyed look and he said, "Yeah, usually we discuss whether to take a case *not* right in front of the client. But for the record, I'm in."

"Me, too," Chris said.

Me, three," Kiley said as if they didn't already know her vote. Jack exchanged a glance with Maya. She nodded with her eyes, and Jack said, "Okay, we'll take the case."

"We need to get our hands on footage of the game." Chris got up and paced a few steps away. "We can put out a request on social, tag the district, and–"

"The coach has footage," Breia said. "He records every game. He sent me the file." She took a thumb drive from her bag. "He doesn't want Ryan on the bench any more than we do. But he didn't have a choice."

"Thumb drive." Kiley leaned over as if to peer inside her purse. "What other spy stuff you got in there?"

"Reusable straw, lip gloss, wallet, this cool little dagger with a scorpion on the handle that I found at a flea market, tissues, breath mints–"

"I want to see the knife," Chris said.

"The knife isn't important. Ryan is," Johnny said, even though he was dying to see it, too. "We'll get on it right now."

"Okay. I um…I better get back. Ryan doesn't know I came to you guys, and I have to figure out how to tell him."

"I have a suggestion," Jack said.

"You can trust him," Chris said in a conspiratorial whisper. "He used to be a shrink."

"I'm still a shr—a psychiatrist." Jack rolled his eyes. "I'm just not practicing as one."

"Please. I'll take any advice I can get."

He nodded. "I don't know your brother, so you're a better judge than I am, but I wonder if it would be easier coming from the guys."

"I agree with Jack," Johnny said, throwing to Chris with a look.

"Yeah, maybe he'll take it better from us," Chris agreed. "We kind of male-bonded over manual labor."

Breia nodded. "Okay. That might work."

"I'll text him and set up a meet," Chris said, yanking out his phone.

"Thank you. I appreciate the help."

"Here, take this way out," Johnny said, and he put a hand on her arm and walked her to the French doors at the back of the library.

While shoveling snow out there, Jack had discovered a flagstone walk under a thin layer of loose soil, weeds and debris. Now that spring was coming, they could clear it off and direct clients to that entry.

He opened the doors, ensuring the path was clear all the way around to the driveway. Kiley wanted to put up framework up to hold grapevines and create a covered walkway. He thought it was a cool idea.

~

"Okay, so what did you see?" Kiley asked.

Maya jerked her gaze away from the view through the French doors of Johnny walking away with the pretty, age-appropriate client. "Nothing. They're not even holding hands."

Kiley glanced at Jack, nodded knowingly and said, "What happened to Johnny by the fireplace?"

Nodded, Maya went back to her stool in front of the computers. "He disappeared. No other word for it. Jack and I both saw it. It wasn't a trick of the light, he was *gone*."

"He was," Jack agreed. "He vanished for about a second. Then he was back." He glanced outside where Maya had been looking.

Johnny came walking back along the path and inside, and Kiley reminded herself she had no real reason to feel pissed at him. Maya was the one getting cold feet about what was obviously simmering between them.

Still, she might've sounded a little pissy when she said, "So what the hell *was* that Johnny?" And just like Maya had, he mistook her meaning.

"What? I just walked her to her car!"

Kiley blinked and gave her head a shake. That *was* what she'd been feeling angry about, on Maya's behalf, though it wasn't her business, except it was. But it was not what she'd been asking. "I mean when Jack and Maya say you... you know... blinked out."

He didn't answer and Jack said, "It was only for a second."

Johnny nodded. "I'm not sure, but I think I might have um... time traveled."

"You did what?" Maya asked, coming closer. Her awkwardness had clearly taken a back seat to her concern.

"It was like Breia's story sucked me in and I was just suddenly there, at Ryan's high school dance, watching it play out in real time."

"Holy..." Chris ran over to the computer bar, sliding onto the stool Maya had vacated.

Her eyes were on Johnny and they were worried.

"This is gonna come in handy!" Chris said, keying in search terms.

"I could control it, too," Johnny said, picking up on Chris's enthusiasm, though at a considerably lesser degree. "I could stop time, rewind, play back, freeze frame."

"Like a living VCR," Jack said.

And Chris asked, "Did you interact with anyone?"

"Yeah, I shouted out to Ryan, and then there was a bouncer up in my face."

"Right, the dreaded high school dance bouncers," Kiley said.

"Chaperone, whatever. I'm telling you, I feel as if I was physically there. I poked the guy and he was solid."

"You poked the bouncer?" Chris asked.

"Well, this is a new development," Jack said. "Isn't it?"

"Brand new," Johnny confirmed. "I'd like to ask my grandfather about it, but he's..." He shook his head like shaking off a fly. "Ryan didn't dump the punch bowl on his girlfriend. Somebody else was there, somebody without a body."

Kiley brought the thumb drive to the back of the room and handed it to Chris at the computer bar. "Let's take a look at that basketball game."

Chris plugged and played. Everyone gathered around, Johnny moving up close beside Maya almost without thinking about it,

Kiley thought. Then he seemed to realize, and backed up a step with a quick sideways look to see if Maya had noticed. She had.

Kiley felt bad for being the first to speak in favor of taking this case. There were clearly sparks between Johnny and Breia, at least on Breia's side. And Maya's nonchalant attitude about her and Johnny was as fake as a New Yorker's tan. Damn, she should have thought it through.

Jack had. She knew it for sure. He had been the only one to hesitate in voting to take Breia and Ryan's case. And that had to be why. Although most of the time he seemed clueless about the sizzle between the two, he sensed enough to be careful with Maya's feelings.

Kiley was starting to think Jack might be more of a catch than she'd at first realized. He was kind of a keeper.

"There it is, there it is." Chris stopped the video, backed up a few frames, clicked to zoom and then slowed down the playback. Everyone leaned in, regardless of who was beside whom.

Ryan and the other player were running down the basketball court, side by side, Ryan with the ball, the other kid trying to stop him, and then suddenly the two of them went flying ass over elbows.

Chris stopped and backed up again, then played again, frame by frame this time.

"Look, look, look, right there," he said. "Look how their backs arch right... *there*." He froze the screen.

"It looks like they're both being shoved from behind," Jack said. "Except there's nothing behind them."

"No, there's something." Johnny leaned in, reaching across Maya to point at the screen right behind the boys, and then he hit the print key. His arm brushed across her chest and he pulled away as if burned.

Kiley rolled her eyes. They were idiots, both of them. She might have to murder them. Slowly, so they'd have time to repent.

Somebody laughed as if amused by her thought, and she turned around, then had a delayed-reaction chill up her spine as she placed the roughshod velvet voice. It was that same laugh she'd heard before.

Slowly, so they'll have time to repent. That's rich. I like you, kid.

And nobody else acted as if they'd heard a thing. She frowned and asked herself if she had maybe imagined the raspy voice in her head, just then.

"He's right," Maya said. "There *is* something, a distortion in the space behind them." She pointed where Johnny had.

The printer churned out a sheet and Johnny grabbed it, moved closer to the window, and held it up in the direct sunlight. Then he went back to the computer bar, snatched a red Sharpie from the cupful of pens, and drew an outline around it, a blob. Then he held it up beside the image on the computer screen. "Does everyone see it now?"

"Oh my God." Kiley touched the screen with a forefinger. "The space within the outline is different from the space outside it. It's kind of... wavery."

"Could be anything," Jack said. "And the footage doesn't show their feet. From the waist up, it's obvious nobody was pushed, but the camera angle is up too high to *prove* nobody was tripped."

"I'll go with Plan A," Chris said. "Put out feelers on social. See if anyone got any footage from other angles."

His phone pinged and he picked it up. "It's Ryan. I texted him about a meetup. He says we're on. The village park in twenty minutes."

Johnny got up and he and Chris headed back through the house and out the front door to meet the young man and try to get him to trust them with his ghost problem. If, indeed, a ghost *was* his problem. Kiley wondered if maybe he was a just a jerk.

She sent Jack a look, inclined her head toward the door, and he picked up the message the way he always did. "I'm gonna go make coffee," he said. "I'll uh—whatever." And then he left her and Maya alone.

Maya had taken over the computer Chris had been using, so Kiley slid up onto the stool next to hers. She was tapping her way through an internet wormhole on teenage hauntings.

"Soooo... this must be awkward for you."

Without looking up or blinking, Maya said, "Not at all."

"Did you notice a little—"

"Chemistry between Johnny and Breia? Yes. I noticed it. You'd have to be blind not to notice." She slid off her stool and paced away. "She's cute and kind of sweet, isn't she?"

It wasn't really a question, and Kiley felt disloyal to say yes, so she said nothing.

"And closer to his age. It's probably for the best. And I can stay professional and objective. It's not a problem. I'm going out for more Fair Trade Coffee. We're down to the last bag and if I wait too long, one of you will replace it with GMO, chemical-laced, ground roast death. See you later."

Kiley held up her hands. "I get it, I get it. And it's fine, I don't do the cry-on-my-shoulder thing worth a crap, anyway. But if you want to spew some venom in a good old-fashioned bitch-fest, I'm your girl."

Maya stopped at the door and looked back at her. "You're a marshmallow in a prickly cactus shell, is what you are. Thanks, Kiley."

Kiley blew her a kiss, but flipped her off at the end. It had the desired affect - Maya smiled. Even though Kiley was pretty sure her heart was hurting.

CHAPTER FIVE

$\mathcal{J}$ ohnny and Chris stood in front of a bench in the little park where the local merchants gathered for lunch, except in winter. They were missing out today, though. It felt like spring. He closed his eyes and said, "Spring's coming early this year."

"Oh yeah? You get another new ability or are you just optimistic?" Chris laughed.

Johnny tried to, but it came out like a gut-punch grunt, and Chris's brows went up and he said, "Sorry. Too soon?"

"No. But that new power—it was scary, to be honest."

"I'd really like to know. And it won't go further."

"I know that."

"I research this stuff, but I'm on the outside looking in," Chris said. "So, it's partly selfish I want to know, but partly–I mean, we're friends. And I can help."

"You think?"

"I can almost always help," Chris said. Then, pushing a hand over his tight braids, "It's what I do. So come on, tell me. What was it like?"

"Like I fell into the past. At first, I didn't know what had

39

happened. I had that falling sensation but only for a second. I got my balance, looked around, saw a decorated school gym full of kids, and then spotted Ryan arguing with a girl. And it hit me that somehow or other, I was there the night it happened. And it felt like I had time traveled, you know? Not like a vision or a dream, but like I was actually there."

"My first thought would be, how the hell do I get back?" Chris said.

"Right after, how the hell did I get here?" Johnny said. "But there was nothing I could do about it right then, so I put all my focus on seeing what really happened that night. And I figured out that I could kind of freeze time and even back it up and slow it down."

"Did Ryan see you?"

"Yeah, through a crowd, though, and it was dark other than the disco ball."

"How long were you there, do you think?"

Johnny shook his head, because when he tried to think of an answer to the question, it started to spin. "I don't know. Five minutes, maybe?"

"But you were only gone a second or less. Which means, you blipped back to real time one second after you blipped out. Maybe no matter how long you spend in the past, you'll always pop back in to a second after you left." He nodded fast, then held up a finger all of the sudden. "Or, maybe for every five minutes you're there, you lose one second here." He started tapping notes on his phone. "Or maybe–"

"Yeah, this is making my head ache."

"Right, right," Chris said.

"And you're right. I kept wondering how the hell I was gonna find my way back to my own time. Or if I even could."

Johnny told himself to stop talking and kind of clenched his jaw. It wasn't like him to spew so many words.

Chris was fascinated, though. "But this time traveling sort of thing never happened before?"

"No."

"Man, I think you need to talk to your grandfather."

"I've been trying."

"Hey, guys." Ryan stood on the sidewalk five feet away.

Johnny lifted a hand in greeting, and he and Chris walked over. Chris and Ryan fist-bumped.

"So, what's up? You got more work for me?"

"We think you might have work for us," Chris said.

Ryan just looked confused. Johnny said, "No lead-up or anything, huh, Chris?" He shook his head and sighed. "Ryan, we think you have a problem. You didn't know this, but Chris and I have a..." He looked at Chris. "What would you call it, a business?"

"A service," Chris said. "We help dead people move on."

Ryan hid his reaction behind a derisive grin, but Johnny saw it anyway. "Wait, wait. Are you talking about that Spook Central shit?" He rolled his eyes. "That's you guys?"

It wasn't surprising he'd heard of them. They'd had some big press between the bodies being found in the fall and the cold case murder they'd solved at Christmastime.

"Us and some others," Chris went on. Johnny was content to let him do the talking. That way he could observe. He wasn't sensing any dead people around, but that was Jack's thing, not his. So he mostly watched Ryan. Behind what he tried to show them, the young man looked tired, maybe depressed.

"We watched the video of that game," Chris said. "We know you didn't push that kid."

He didn't get angry, just sighed. "How do you even know about all that?" Then he finally lifted his chin a little, met their eyes. "My sister?"

Chris nodded. "We can help."

"You gotta be kidding me." Ryan shook his head, backing

away from them. "I thought you guys were okay, but you're just a couple of crooks out to con my sister."

"It's not like that!" Chris said.

Johnny held up his hands palms up. "We're not conning anyone, Ryan. But maybe we can help."

"You wanna help? I'll tell you how to help. Stay the *hell* away from my sister!" Then he turned and strode back the way he'd come, out of the park onto the sidewalk, headed across the street. He was so angry, he bumped into a guy coming toward him in the crosswalk, catching him on the shoulder. The guy's coffee splashed all over his coat and he turned around and punched Ryan right in the jaw.

Johnny and Chris both shouted and ran toward the street. Ryan staggered three steps and fell down near the curb, and the guy took one step toward him. And then a truck veered out of its lane and hit the guy.

Just like that. "Oh hell!" Johnny shouted while Chris brought his arm up over his face and cringed. The sound was awful, a crunching thud. The guy flew, and when he hit the pavement, his head split open.

People came out of nearby businesses to join those who'd already been outside.

Johnny and Chris were already in the street, so they went around the crowd to Ryan. He was still down, half over the curb, half in the road, propped up on one elbow. He was staring at the dead man, his eyes just about bulging.

"Hey, hey, look at me," Johnny said. "Look at me." And when Ryan did, "Are you okay?"

He just shook his head, left, then right. He was trembling. He looked at Chris, then Johnny again. "Please be for real. I need you to be for real." And then he just started sobbing.

CHAPTER SIX

*J*ohnny put an arm around Ryan and started walking, but then he stopped and looked back. There were security cameras on the entrances of most of the businesses. The police would have footage.

Jeannie, owner of the Village Cafe was standing in her doorway. She said, "Boys, I don't know that you should leave the scene."

"The kid's hurt," Johnny said. "Tell the cops we'll come in and give statements as soon as—"

"You can tell them yourself," a woman said. Johnny turned and saw Lieutenant Mendosa.

"You got here quick."

"I was around the corner." She tilted her head and said, "How's your grandfather?"

"He was good last time we spoke. This is Ryan Sousa, and he barely avoided getting hit by that truck himself."

"After the victim punched him in the face," she said, nodding at Ryan's swollen jaw.

"He had nothing to do with that guy getting hit," Chris said, then belatedly added, "Christophe with a C H, a P H, and an E."

"I know your full name, Chris," Mendosa said. "It's not like you spook hunters aren't constantly tangled up in my cases."

"Look, you can see the whole thing for yourself," Johnny said. He knew he was acting overly protective of Ryan. The kid was seventeen. But he was also a mess. "There must be five cameras that captured what happened, including the one you have there to catch crosswalk violators." Johnny nodded at the camera right above the crosswalk button on the corner. "Ryan had nothing to do with it, but he's underage, traumatized, and hurt. Let me take him home."

"Mm-hm. That's a reasonable request, except that a man is dead." They all turned toward where the man was lying dead in the street. Johnny caught a glimpse of his head between the onlookers and had to turn away. Paramedics were piling out of their truck, but the dead guy was beyond their help.

"How bad are you hurt, Ryan?" Lieutenant Mendosa asked.

"Not very bad," he said.

"Anything broken? Bleeding? Potential internal injuries? Did you hit your head when you landed?"

Ryan kept shaking his head no to each question.

"So, then you're perfectly capable of answering a few questions at my desk, which is two blocks that way, right?"

"You're taking him in for questioning?" Johnny asked.

"He's been on the scene of five violent incidents," she said. "Always against somebody who has been in conflict with him in some way. You think I shouldn't be curious about that?"

"Fine. We're coming with him."

"We are?" Chris asked.

"Until his sister takes over, at least," Johnny said.

Chris met his eyes, swallowed hard and said, "Okay."

Johnny sat in a chair in front of the Lieutenant's desk. Chris had opted to wait out front for Breia to arrive, and said he'd fill the gang in while he was at it.

The office was small, the chairs were hard. Mendosa's desk was decorated with file folders and coffee stains.

"Is it true what the onlookers told me?" asked, taking her seat. "That guy punched you in the face in the crosswalk right before he got hit?"

Ryan nodded.

"Did you know him?"

"No."

"So, why'd he punch you?"

"I bumped into him in the crosswalk. His coffee spilled. It was an accident. He spun me around and punched me in the jaw."

"We saw the whole thing," Johnny said. "It happened just like he says it did. Chris will tell you the same. And I hate to say it, but that guy needed an ass-kicking. Maybe not by a *truck*, but—"

Mendosa sent him a quelling glance and returned to grilling the teen. "He punched you in the face, and then what?"

"I went flying and landed on the curb, right by the newspaper box." He rose from his chair, turned around and lifted his jacket and shirt. There was a streak of road rash and a purple bruise had already formed."

She winced, reached for a button on her phone and said "Wendy, send somebody in here with an ice pack." And then to Ryan, "I'm sorry kid. I'm not gonna keep you here long, promise. Tell me the rest."

He faced front again, clothes in place, but he didn't sit. "Then the truck hit him," Ryan said. "He flew so fast it was like he was shot out of a cannon. And then he hit the road and his head just..." He spread his hand open, fingers splayed. "Splat." His shoulders were shaking, and he turned around, putting his back to both adults in the room.

"That's exactly what happened," Johnny said. "I saw it all, and so did everyone else there. And so did the cameras."

Then Ryan seemed to have himself together enough to face them again. But when he did, his eyes widened, and focused past Lieutenant Mendosa's left shoulder. She looked behind her as he said, "It's okay. Leave her alone, I mean it!"

"Easy, Ryan." Johnny got up and put both hands on his shoulders. "I've got you."

"I'm sorry," Mendosa said, but she was sending worried looks from the kid to Johnny, like she was figuring out that maybe he wasn't okay after all. "Who were you talking to, Ryan?"

"Nobody." He shoved his hands in his pockets and hunched into his hoodie like he was cold.

And then the window behind Mendosa exploded. She shouted and bolted around the desk. Ryan turned and ran out of the office, and bumped right into Breia and Jack, who'd just come in.

But he didn't stop, and he didn't run out the front door. He went the other way, down a hall and around a corner, as they all went after him. Mendosa shouted orders. "Somebody just smashed my window! Get on it. I've got this."

They rounded a corner. There were cells, just five of them. Nobody occupied any of them, but the one on the end was open and apparently being used for storage. That was where Ryan was huddled in a corner with his knees drawn to his chest, shaking.

"Ryan!" Breia ran into the cell and dropped to her knees beside him, hugging his shoulders. "Baby what's wrong? What did they do to you?"

He muttered something only she could hear.

"Sure he's safe in there," Jack said, to empty space on his left. "But he can't stay there forever."

Johnny tipped his head and said, "Who you talking to, Jack?"

"The janitor, he said…. Ohhhh." He looked to his left, again. "I get it.".

Mendosa said, "We don't use that cell. The inmates complain.

46

Say somebody touches them in the night. You know, a hand to the shoulder or back, nothing nasty." She eyed Jack. "So, if you have something to tell me–"

"Maintenance man named Jerry, according to the patch on his pocket."

"Uh-huh," she said.

Jack shrugged. "We're busy right now but give us a call if you need us. You have the number." Then he looked inside the cell. "You ready to go, Ryan?"

"Mr. McCain, do you have any idea who smashed my office window just now?" Mendosa eyed him suspiciously.

"I'm pretty sure it was the parents of that pair in the cell," he said.

"I'll have them brought in for–"

"Can't. Cause, they're dead."

"And the janitor?"

"Him too. Doesn't seem menacing, though."

"Right," she said. No inflection and her face was inscrutable.

Ryan got up on his feet. Breia kept her arm around his shoulders and walked him out of the cell and down the hall.

As they drew near, Mendosa said, "I'm sorry, Ryan. I should've realized how shaken up you were."

Then, to Breia, "Go ahead and take him home. I'll be in touch. I have everyone's info." She fished out a card and handed it to Breia.

As they walked out, Johnny hung back.

"What's up?" Mendosa asked, because it was obvious something was.

"My grandfather took off to visit friends in Florida he said. But I haven't been able to reach him for a few days and I'm getting worried."

She nodded slow. "I'm very fond of John Redhawk," she said. "He leave you an address?"

"Yeah."

"Text it to me. I'll have somebody check on him."

"You'll have it in an hour. Thank you."

She nodded.

Johnny and Chris walked Ryan back to the truck and took him back to Kiley's house, where his sister was waiting.

Breia asked Johnny to drive them home, and he couldn't very well say no. But he tapped Chris to come along. Breia and Ryan lived in a little white two-story house with sea-green shutters with heart cutouts and window boxes currently only full of dirt. It had a neat sidewalk bordered in plants, some of which were already a couple of inches high and bore tightly closed buds.

The inside consisted of an eat-in kitchen, a cozy living room, a staircase, and presumably a bathroom somewhere. Johnny and Chris sat at Breia's kitchen table. It was square and white with a matching chair on each side. The whole kitchen was white, but she'd used red checkered curtains, dish towels, and potholders to match the red ceramic cabinet knobs and drawer pulls. The toaster and teapot were red, too.

Ryan was in the living room, on the sofa, with an ice pack on his jaw and another on his back. Breia poured four glasses of iced tea. Chris took two, and carried one in to Ryan.

"So, first things first, I guess," Johnny said. He pulled up the image of the punch bowl incident. It had been sent to Chris online, someone at the dance randomly snapped a photo in that direction at the moment it had happened.

"There's something behind the table. You can see how the space is the slightest bit off." He showed the image to Briea, and glanced into the next room where Chris was showing the same image to Ryan. Ryan rolled his eyes.

"Same thing at the basketball game," Johnny went on.

48

Chris interrupted at that point. "He's burying the lead. I asked for everybody's footage online, and one of those shots has you guys head to toe at the moment of the fall. Nobody is pushing anybody. Nobody you can see, anyway." He turned his phone toward Ryan.

"Here," Johnny added, finding the image on his own device and showing it to Briea. "In this shot, I outlined it. Just look at the difference between within the line, and without. Same as with the image at the punch bowl." He flipped images and held out the phone.

"So what?" Ryan asked.

"Here," Chris said, scrolling his phone, then pushing it at the kid again.

"I think we're overwhelming him," Johnny said.

"This is the blown-up, zoomed in, frame-by-frame footage of the basketball game," Chris rushed on as he tapped the play button. Ryan watched this time. And there just came this look of hatred over his face.

Chris said, "Ryan, are you seeing something different in the footage than we are?"

Ryan pressed his lips but didn't speak. Johnny and Breia rose and moved closer to the sofa, and Chris showed them the video he'd just shown the kid.

"Come on, man," Chris said. "Do you want help or not? What have you got to lose by letting us try?"

At last, Ryan nodded, and his eyelashes were wet. "I can see them."

Breia gasped, then clapped her hand over her mouth.

Johnny moved around the sofa, took the easy chair nearest Ryan, and leaned forward, elbows on his knees.

"Then, do you know who's haunting you?" Johnny asked.

"Yeah," he said. "It's..." He looked over the back of the sofa at his sister. "I'm sorry, Breia. It's our parents."

MAGGIE SHAYNE

"No, it's not." Her denial seemed like a reflex. "I mean, it can't be. They wouldn't... they wouldn't *hurt* anybody."

"They killed that guy today," Ryan said.

A silence fell over them all, until Breia whispered, "How?"

"They were in the truck. They turned the wheel. I saw them and I c-c-couldn't stop it." Ryan's lips pulled into a wide grimace and his shoulders shook harder, but not one tear escaped. "They dumped the punch bowl on Kristin. They shoved that kid who kept fouling me on the court. And that fire last week, in principal Gordon's garage? I think they did that too. He'd told me off that day for rough-housing in the hall."

Breia got up and left the room. They heard rattling, and when she came back, she had a bottle of pills in her hand. "Take what the doctor prescribed you for stress." The shook a tablet from the bottle and pressed it into his hand. Hers was shaking. "Stress and anxiety. No freaking wonder. God, Ryan, you should've told me."

"I didn't think you'd believe me."

"Of course I believe you! Take the pill."

He lifted his head and met his sister's eyes. "You're the one under stress. Because of me. You don't even smile anymore."

"Take the med. You need to rest. Take it."

"There's more to tell them, Breia."

"It'll take time to work. You can tell them while you wait. If they can get rid of–"

"Shhhh!" He sat back in his chair, looking at a spot just past them. Then he lunged off the couch and snatched the pill bottle from his sister's hand, ripped off the cap, and said, "I'll take them all, I swear to God, I'll take them all right now if you do *anything* to them!"

"Ryan, no!" Breia cried.

Johnny felt a chill right up his spine so real that he got to his feet and turned around. The menacing presence was undeniable, and yet invisible. It was all around them, surging and rippling but he couldn't see a thing. He felt it.

"I think we should continue this discussion at our place," Chris said with a look at Johnny. "Maya's been working her magic over there. You guys really need to see it." He spoke as if the ghosts were listening.

He was right, though, Johnny thought. Maya had been magicking the hell out of Spook Central. Kiley had been pretty freaked by the ghosts in her place, and then just when they thought they had them all cleared out, another one had shown up at the door.

There was something about the house that attracted them. That was Johnny's theory. Chris agreed, and thought it was because of all the deaths that had happened there, but Johnny felt like it might be something older. Ghosts or not, Kiley loved the house, and she'd sunk her last penny into it. She wouldn't give it up, even if she could. So Maya had taken on the task of keeping Spook Central spook-free.

Breia moved around the sofa and closer to Johnny.

"Are they right here?" she asked. "Mom? Dad? Is this really you? Why? Why would you do these things?"

The lights blazed brighter and one of the bulbs right over her head popped so loudly she ducked and covered her head with her arms.

Johnny wrapped his arms around Breia, protecting her with his body. It was knee-jerk, not planned. In the dim room, she looked up and into his eyes. He smiled nervously and straightened, brushing bits of light bulb glass from her hair. "Trust me on this. Come back with us. Okay?"

"Okay."

"It won't matter," Ryan said. "They stick to me, wherever I go. There's nowhere they can't be."

"God, Ryan, how long has this been going on?" Breia put an arm around her brother, and they walked to the door. She grabbed her coat and purse off a nearby hook. Ryan was still wearing his, but he snagged his backpack as they passed it on the floor.

"As long as I can remember," he said.

Johnny said, "Maybe pack an overnight bag. Just in case."

"Do you think we can do that, Ryan?" Brica asked, wide-eyed.

"They won't hurt us, just anyone who tries to hurt us or... you know, keep them away from me." He sent a warning look to Johnny and Chris.

"Good thing there's nobody here like that." Chris looked around and laughed nervously.

The siblings headed upstairs. Johnny felt on guard the whole time. He felt under watch, and when he sent Chris a questioning look, Chris nodded. He felt it, too. He could hear them moving around upstairs, but other than that the house was quiet. No trouble. So far, so good.

Then why were the hairs on his nape bristling?

They came down with their bags and the four of them headed outside. Breia closed and locked the door behind them and turned to look at her brother with tears in her eyes. "I can't believe you never told me."

"It wasn't a big deal." He pushed his hair off his forehead. "They used to be way nicer."

They all walked together, moving carefully and quickly, but not running, as if any sudden movement might set the dead people off. Johnny was looking around the whole time, he and Chris flanking Breia and Ryan as if they could protect them.

But Breia and Ryan were probably not the ones in need of protection, he thought with a shiver.

They made it all the way to Johnny's big white EV truck. Goosebumps were rising on his forearms.

"They won't stop us," Ryan said. "They don't care where we go. They go wherever I go, so it doesn't matter." As if to prove it, he climbed into Johnny's pickup, taking the slender rear seat.

Briea said, "I can't believe they would hurt us. If this is really them, I mean." She looked around as if she might see them.

"You don't think it's really them?" Johnny asked.

Chris climbed into the back seat with Ryan and closed the door. Johnny opened the front passenger side, and helped Breia up. She was four inches shorter than Maya, who could hop in and out of his truck with ease.

"I think something is happening," she said, settling into her seat, fastening her belt. "Something I don't understand. But I don't believe it's our dead parents. They never hurt anyone in their lives. They were overprotective, if anything."

Johnny got in and drove them toward Kiley's place with more care than he'd ever driven anywhere in his life. It was only a couple of miles. But nothing happened, all the way there. He pulled right into the driveway. All good. Shut off the motor. Still nothing. But everything in him prickled all the same.

"Let's get out and go inside," he said, including the two in the back with his eyes. "Don't knock, it isn't locked, just go in, quick as you can, but carefully."

"I told you, they don't care where we go," Ryan said.

"Yeah, well, if what my... friend Maya did worked, they're gonna care about this," Johnny replied. And even he heard the pride in his voice. "On three, ready? One, two..." On three, he opened the door and jumped out.

Ryan got out from the back, and suddenly the wind came up. out of nowhere. The bottles hanging from the elm tree on the front lawn started swinging and clanging against each other. "Go!"

He pushed the kid ahead of him, relieved when Chris and Breia came around the truck's nose and joined them on the porch stairs. One of the tree bottles smashed into another, and both exploded to bits. And then it happened again, and then again.

Chris swung the front door open and stumbled through it with Ryan under his arm. A flowerpot came flying at them, and

53

Johnny pushed Breia out of its way by a whisper. It smashed the doorframe beside her as they stumbled through the front door together.

The door slammed shut behind them as if it was spring-loaded.

CHAPTER SEVEN

Five Minutes Earlier...
"A rare, quiet moment," Jack said. I can hardly believe it." He slid up behind the sofa, curled his hands over Kiley's shoulders, and dropped a kiss on the top of her head. She felt warm all the way to her toes, and smiled softly, content as a cat.

She'd just sent their newfound video footage of the basketball game, and the punch bowl incident at the dance to the coach, the board of education, and Lieutenant Mendosa. Ryan had done nothing wrong.

Mendosa had just texted back. The police had reached the same conclusion and closed the case. The school was afraid of a civil suit. But Mendosa said releasing the footage to the press would eliminate any risk of that, a very broad hint to Kiley, a journalist.

She'd just uploaded it to the Burnt Hills Gazette's website. Ryan was vindicated.

"Aw, man. I hear the guys pulling in," Jack said. Because he could tell who had arrived according to the sound of their engine, or in Johnny's case, the lack of sound. If it wasn't so sexist, she'd say it must be a guy thing. "Never a dull moment, huh? I wanted to talk."

And Kiley's warm feeling turned to a chill. "You? Talk? About what?" She got off the couch and turned to face him.

"Us," he said. "Is it storming outside?"

They reached the foyer just as the door burst open and Chris came stumbling through, bent low with a young Ryan Sousa on his arm and some kind of windstorm raging at his back.

Johnny came right behind them, his arm around their new client, who looked terrified. Something whipped past her head, damn near braining her just before the two made it inside.

As they stumbled across the threshold, Maya came running from the office skidded to a halt, flung up her hands and shouted "*CLOSE!*"

The door slammed shut.

"Ho-*lee* hell!" Kiley gaped at Maya. "I did not know you could do that."

"*I* did not know I could do that," she replied, looking at her hands like she'd never seen them before.

The four new arrivals were straightening up from their frightened crouches, looking around as if they expected a dragon to bite their heads off momentarily.

"Someone care to fill us in?" Kiley asked.

The teenager, who had to be Breia's brother Ryan, looked at the closed door and whispered, "How are they not in here?"

"I should start at the beginning," Johnny said.

"That's gonna take too long. Let me summarize," Chris interrupted. Breia was right about her brother being haunted. He's been fan-stalked by his dead parents his whole life, probably ever since they died, since they apparently never left. They were nice at first, but now anybody who crosses Ryan gets hurt. Physically hurt. Like when they killed a guy today. With a truck."

Kiley opened her mouth, then closed it again.

"How are they not in here?" Ryan asked again.

"Because," Maya said. "They can't cross the magic circle I cast around this place, enforced by wards and magic." Her voice had a mystical tone and cadence, but then in a perfectly ordinary way, she said, "I'm Maya. Resident Witch. Merry meet."

Ryan looked from her, to the door, as if processing what he had just seen. Then his face sort of softened into a look of innocent hope and he said, "You guys are for real."

"Yeah," Maya said. "We're for real. We've got you, kid. This isn't our first dance with the dead." She frowned, and said, "That was good, I need to jot that down."

~

The storm had ceased as soon as they'd come inside. Kiley and Breia had tossed some munchies into the oven when Breia whispered, "I've never seen my brother this relaxed."

They had a clear line of sight through the dining room to where Ryan and Chris were in animated discussion in the living room. The kid's demeanor had changed entirely. It was as if somebody had turned on the lights.

"I think you two should stay here while we figure this out," Kiley said. "We have extra rooms. And I'm feeling like this sort of thing is probably what they're for."

"You want to play?" Chris asked, his voice carrying from the living room. "C'mon, you're gonna love our setup. State of the art." He and Ryan went around the bottom of the staircase, down the hallway toward the office.

When the timer went off, there were frozen pizzas and Vegan buffalo wings enough for a crowd. Jack carried in an armload of everything that could, in its wildest dreams, serve as dipping sauce, and began lining them up on the table.

Kiley sent him a look. He said, "What? I wanted to give everybody options."

Johnny liked how they were with each other. He wondered if

they realized how connected they were. You'd know they were a couple, even in a crowd. He wanted that, someday.

His eyes were drawn to Maya's. She was on the other side of the table, filling her plate, and she felt his eyes on her and looked back. He offered a slight smile. She smiled back a little bit, and then Breia took the side next to him, and Maya blinked.

"I'm gonna take all this delish vegan junk food up to my room. I have a ton of social media to catch up. Thank you for cooking Kiley and Breia. Goodnight."

It was a good excuse, Johnny thought, because it was true 100% of the time in her line of work. He was disappointed. And then he wondered if maybe she was trying to get out of Breia's way, and that made him feel as if he were being manipulated. He could decide for himself who he wanted to spend time with.

And then for some reason, he up and blurted, "Anybody want to watch a movie?" while wiping his fingers with a napkin. He headed for the sofa, sank onto it, and stretched his sock-covered feet out in front of him.

Breia said, "I haven't had a night this relaxing since... Ever. Yes, I want to watch a movie."

Uh-oh. He'd messed up.

"I think we're gonna head upstairs," Kiley said. "There's popcorn in the kitchen if you want it. You know where stuff is, Johnny."

Oh shit. He'd really messed up.

"Breia got up. "Thank you. For letting us stay."

Kiley said, "Listen, you don't have to leave until we fix your problem. This place is huge, and...I don't know, I think it likes you."

She took Jack's hand, and he said, "Night, Breia. Night Johnny."

"Night," they returned in unison, and then Johnny said, "What movie?" His throat had gone dry.

"You pick," Breia replied, sitting on the loveseat beside him instead of in any of the other available spots. Maybe Chris and Ryan would get sick of gaming and join them. Although, not if you went by the exclamations and laughter spilling out from the office.

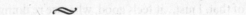

When they reached the top of the stairs, Kiley squeezed Jack's hand and said, "Jeeze, I hope nothing happens between them tonight. Not with Maya in the same house."

"How would she know?" Jack whispered back.

"Oh, she'd know. Did you *see* that door thing she did? That was freaking—"

"That *was* something," he agreed. Then he frowned. "And Johnny has something new, too."

"Understatement of the year, much?" She thought of the woman with the sexy raspy voice that no one else seemed to hear. She couldn't explain it. It wasn't imaginary, and if it had been a hallucination, she'd have had others, wouldn't she?

She undressed and slid into bed. "That was a freak windstorm when they came crashing in, wasn't it?"

He glanced her way and smiled. "I don't think it was a storm." Then he went in to brush his teeth.

When he came back out, she said, "What did you want to talk about, earlier? You said *Us*. Are we okay?"

"Oh, *hell* yes. I mean I am. I'm *way* okay."

She sighed like it was her final breath.

"Are *you* okay?" he asked. "This is all turning out a lot different from what you thought you wanted. Space. Privacy. Independence."

"What I wanted changed." She closed her eyes for a second. "Did you see Ryan when he came through that door? He was devastated."

"Johnny said he threatened suicide to keep the ghosts off them, and he wasn't entirely sure it was an empty threat."

"That poor kid."

"I know."

"We can help him, Jack. You can help him, and I get to be part of that. I just…it feels good, what we're doing."

He smiled. "I'm really glad to hear all that. However. um, I meant, are you okay about us? This, here." He moved his hand back and forth between them. "Johnny's renting my place. It's feeling real now."

She slid her palms up his chest in sexy slow-mo. "I am so okay about us that I didn't think I needed to tell you how very okay I am about us."

He frowned, pretending to translate her longwinded declaration in his head. "So you're good with us?"

"I'm good with us." She kissed his chin. "I'm considerably better than good with us."

"Okay."

"That's what you wanted to talk about?" she asked.

"Uh-huh."

"I prefer to show you instead of tell you. Can I change my answer?"

"No, but you can add notes."

Smiling, she pushed him back onto the pillows and pounced.

CHAPTER EIGHT

*J*ohnny and Breia sat on the love seat, really close, and he was pretty sure she was waiting for him to put his arm around her, but he wasn't going to. He didn't want to start anything up with Maya right upstairs. They'd been sort friendly and flirty and working up to something more not long ago, and even though she seemed to have cooled toward him, it felt like it would be disrespectful.

Then Breia took his wrist in her hand, pulled it around her shoulders, and scooched closer.

Johnny picked a movie and they watched for a while, and during a lull in the action he said. "Tell me about your parents."

She leaned her head back against his arm. Her hair smelled like coconut.

"They were so in love that I sometimes felt like I was in the way of it. A third wheel that came between them."

"They couldn't have felt that way, though." He paused the movie.

"Mom died sixteen weeks after Ryan's birth. Complications from the delivery. An infection. Something. I didn't understand,

61

being only ten years old myself. Dad had a heart attack three months later. Literally died of a broken heart."

He swore softly. "I'm really sorry, Breia."

"The parents I knew were kind, even though they were too obsessed with each other to be very attentive to me. All that changed when Ryan was born. He came early, there were problems. He nearly died. They were completely obsessed with him, by his side twenty-four seven, even while he was still in the hospital. And after he came home, they never left him alone, not even when he was asleep, and they forbade anyone else to touch him, including me."

Johnny was quiet for a long moment, and then he said, "Apparently, they're still that obsessed with him."

"I just can't believe it's them." She turned and pressed her face to his shoulder, sobbing softly. He patted the back of her head a few times.

A throat cleared, and he craned his neck. Maya had come downstairs. She was in purple flannel pajamas with flying witches and yellow moons all over them, and she had a book in her hand. "I'm really sorry. Um... Yeah, I'm sorry, never mind, it can wait."

"No, please," Breia said. She sat up straight and Johnny took the opportunity to pull his arm away. "If you've found anything, I want to know." She brushed the tears from her cheeks.

Maya said, "I don't want to interrupt your movie." She glanced at the TV screen. The movie was paused. And then she stood very still and her face went all soft and sweet. "You're watching *My Cousin Vinny*?" Her eyes shot right to Johnny's.

He shrugged, picked up the remote and returned the TV to the home screen.

Maya came the rest of the way in and sat in one of the chairs, opened the book, a really old looking one with a tattered cover.

"Is that leather-bound? Doesn't that go against your veganism?" Johnny asked.

"The cow was already dead when the book came to me." She shrugged. "But to be honest, you're right. I have been struggling over it. I'd like to replace the cover, but this book is an artifact. So I'm torn. Anyway..." She cleared her throat and smoothed the page. And then she began to read, "'When trap'd a dead man's spirit be, a rend is torn 'twix he and HE.'"

She paused there, then looked up thoughtfully. "The second he is in caps. Get it?" Then she read on. "'For when the body cease to be, the soul must to the Source then flee. The longer they refuse to go, the longer doth the rend then grow, until the pain they undergo erases all they once did know. And so without a body's brain nor Source's mind, the ghost remains, a form gone mad that may attack and with the solid interact. The madness and the pow'r increase until their energy's release.'"

She lifted her head. "A soul belongs either in the body, or on the other side, united with the Whole. A soul in between is unmoored and in pain. It grows angrier and more powerful over time, to the point where it can move physical things. Like punch-bowls and basketball players."

"And trucks," Johnny said softly.

"Then it really could be them? Breia asked. "My parents actually killed that man?"

"I don't think it matters who they used to be," Maya said. "They aren't that anymore."

Breia closed her eyes, lowered her head.

"We're going to help them," Johnny said. "We are."

"We are," Maya said. "I just thought...you should know."

Johnny thought he got it. When Maya stumbled onto a clue in a case, she could never share it fast enough. Keeping it to herself until morning would've been impossible.

"I really am sorry I interrupted," she said. Johny wasn't though. "I'm just gonna fade into the woodwork now."

"Oh. Yeah. You blend," Johnny said exactly as Morisa Tomei had said two minutes ago in the film.

She stopped backing up and looked at him and smiled and her lips kind of trembled. Then she turned and headed upstairs in her purple flannel Halloween jammies.

"I think I'm going to turn in, too," Breia said. She slid off the sofa. "Goodnight, Johnny. Thank you for everything."

"Night."

She went upstairs. Johnny settled back, picked up the remote, and resumed the movie.

~

When Kiley came downstairs freshly loved and showered, she heard laughter from the kitchen and followed the mouthwatering smells that wafted out with it. Johnny and Breia were out there, cooking up a storm.

"Hey, just in time!" Johnny grabbed a mug, filled it with coffee and put it into Kiley's hand. "Breia wanted to show her appreciation by making us all breakfast. She asked for my help finding her way around the kitchen."

"Awww. That's sweet of you guys."

"Is anyone else up yet?" Breia slid four more pancakes onto one of the stacks. "I can keep it warm in the oven, if–"

"Don't worry," Kiley said. "The aroma is working its way upstairs as we speak—"

"What smells so good?" Chris asked, arriving in the kitchen in blue PJs with gold piping and cozy looking slippers. When he looked at the platters on the counter, his eyes lit up. Chris loved food.

"Let's get it on the table, then." Johnny took a stack of plates from the cabinet to the dining room. Chris followed suit, handling silverware, maple syrup and butter. Breia carried a platter heaped with pancakes in one hand, and hash browns in the other. So Kiley grabbed the sausage in her free hand and carried her coffee.

Maya came down while they were putting stuff on the table, and said, "Oh, wow." She was dressed for the day. Only Chris remained in pajamas. "That looks great." But she went straight through, returning with a full coffee mug to take the seat next to Kiley. Johnny was across from them, Breia next to him, and Chris took the far end.

Maya looked at all the offerings, reached for the hash browns, put a scoop on her plate, and picked up her fork.

"Oh, no, Maya, you can eat all of it," Breia said.

"No, I'm—"

"I know, you're vegan. Johnny helped me make everything. The pancakes are egg and dairy-free, and the sausage is plant-based."

She looked across at Johnny. He shrugged. "The sausage was in the freezer. We cooked all of it. Hope that's okay."

"That was… Yes, it's okay. That's what it was in there for. I'm gonna um… " She got up. "We need more coffee in here, huh?" She went to the kitchen.

Jack chose that moment to come trotting down the stairs yelling, "You all better have saved me some of what smells so good." He came straight to the table and took the end chair to Kiley's left. "Oh, man, this all looks great." He sat down and dug in.

"Save some for Ryan," Chris called.

"I have it covered," Breia said. "It's been so long since he's had a good night's rest, I hope he sleeps straight through til lunch. So I put a plate aside for him in case he does."

Kiley said, "Be right back," and trailed her hand over Jack's as she slid her chair out and headed for the kitchen.

Maya was pouring coffee into a thermal carafe. Kiley could only see her back, except when she glanced over her shoulder to see who it was.

"That was thoughtful, them making breakfast," Kiley said as a lame effort to open conversation.

"I didn't know Johnny knew how to make vegan pancakes," Maya said. She had to clear her throat halfway through.

"He's full of surprises."

"He is," she said. She screwed the lid on the carafe and put a fresh pot on to brew.

Kiley got enough mugs for everyone in two hands.

"Looks like they're really hitting it off, doesn't it?" Maya asked softly. She was standing in front of the fridge, holding its door open and staring inside like she'd blanked on what she'd been after.

"Johnny and Breia?" Kiley asked.

"Yeah. It's okay. I'm glad. She's sweet."

"Just not this soon," Kiley said. "I mean, that's what I'd be feeling. Like, dude, already? I haven't even changed the sheets since the last time we–"

"I told you, we never even kissed."

"I'm sorry. I shouldn't have — I shouldn't be a smart-ass about this. Nor should I keep butting in."

"No, it's...fine. And you don't even have to share intimate details about you and Jack in return."

Kiley grinned. "You don't know what you're missing. It's good. Maybe a little too good."

"No such thing."

"There is for me. Too good is scary. It's like waiting for the axe to fall."

Maya tilted her head to one side. "There's only an axe if you think there's an axe."

"Okay, *Sensei*. Can you get the creamer?"

"Got it."

They headed back to the dining room and passed the caffeine around, and soon they were rubbing their bellies and leaning back in their chairs.

"I'm going upstairs to check on Ryan," Breia said. She left to a chorus of "thanks for breakfast," and "breakfast was great" sorts of declarations.

"While they're upstairs," Maya said, "I found something in that book that arrived yesterday."

"*Souls Entrapped Between the Worlds*," Johnny said. "Author, unknown." He shared her love of magical tomes.

"Allegedly translated from a book smuggled out of the Alexandrian Library before it burned," Maya added, her eyes excited. "There's a spell for binding a soul to its body. We need to lure them to their graves and cast the spell there."

"And how would we do that?" Johnny asked.

"Contagious sample from their offspring would do it," she said. "Blood would be best."

"Wait, wait, you want blood from Breia and Ryan?" Kiley said.

Johnny realized he'd kind of forgotten anyone else was in the room.

"Just a little." Maya held up a thumb and forefinger, nearly touching. And then she said, "I need to be the one to go."

"Not alone, you're not," Johnny said. "I'll go with you."

Chris looked at his empty plate and cup, and said, "Not being fond of graveyards, I'll man the office."

"I'll stay here, too," Kiley said. "We only need the ones with abilities to check out the jail cell." Then she grinned. "The Woo-Woo Crew. Jack, Maya, and Johnny should go." Then she frowned. "If they *can* go."

Everyone looked toward the front door at the same time, and the tension in the room stretched tight.

"Well, that's the question of the day, isn't it?" Jack said, his voice so low it was like he didn't want the ghosts to hear him. "Will Ryan's ghosts attack as soon as we try to leave the house?"

"I think the only way to know is to try," Johnny said. "Get the kids down here."

Nodding, Chris said, "I'll pull up their burial info on the net and get you a map with the graves marked, to save time."

Maya said, "I'm going to expand the circle all the way to the edges of the front and back lawns and include the driveway."

"And I'm going to brush my teeth!" Kiley announced. "Break!"

Everyone laughed and the tension eased. Chris headed for the office. Johnny went upstairs. Maya watched Johnny go upstairs.

Kiley sent Jack an "Are you seeing this?" look, her wide eyes indicating the pair of them.

Jack followed her gaze, but with a "wtf are you talking about?" expression in his own eyes.

Men!

CHAPTER NINE

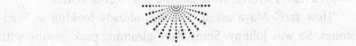

The ghosts hadn't done anything when Johnny, Jack, and Maya had walked outside and got into the van. Jack took the driver's seat. Maya climbed into the passenger seat up front, forcing Johnny to get in the back.

It was so quiet when they pulled out, that Johnny wondered if the ghosts were gone for good.

Jack drove them forty-five miles away, out in the countryside where a cemetery so well-groomed it would make a golf course jealous, sprawled out in three directions.

Jack parked on the street and shut off the van. Johnny opened the back doors and got down. He went around to offer Maya a hand, but she'd hopped to the pavement before he could try.

It was midday, but the sky was moody and dark and the wind was as cold as winter. Johnny had two gauze pads in a zipper bag. Each one held a few drops of blood and a couple strands of Breia's and Ryan's hair. Maya had a bag like a steampunk physician might carry. Brown canvas with pleather trim and way more buckles and straps than it could possibly need.

Patches of snow still hugged the bottom of the wrought iron

fence that marked the front of the graveyard. It had a tall, elaborate iron arch with a small gate that hung a little crookedly.

Johnny pulled out the map Chris had printed for them. "This way," he said, heading through the gate and angling left, with Jack and Maya on either side of him.

They walked through last winter's wilted grass and old decayed leaves leftover from fall, too wet to even skitter.

"How far?" Maya asked. She was already looking at headstones. So was Johnny. Some were gleaming pink granite with elegant engraving. Some even had images of the deceased. And there were small blocks that barely rose a foot above the ground and old stones engraved with weird skulls that had bones underneath, like pirate flags. Others had less skeletal faces with wings on either side or oblong faces that might've been demons or ghosts or possibly angels. Death angels.

"They're known as death's head symbols," Maya said. Because she noticed him looking, he thought, the way she noticed so many things about him. That was a good sign, right?

"They seem pretty dark."

"The Puritan view of death was that it was a punishment for original sin," Maya said. "They feared it. The death's head is thought to have been a reminder to the living not to sin, for death and judgment await them, too."

Jack said, "Fear. The greatest motivator."

"How far, Johnny?" Maya asked again, because he had never answered. He noticed her voice wobbled a little.

"I'm not sure. Breia hasn't been back here since the funeral and she was only ten. And Ryan's never been here."

"That's odd, isn't it?" Jack said. "There's gotta be a reason behind that. Then again, it's an hour away."

Johnny nodded in agreement, but his focus was on Maya. "You're not okay here, are you?"

"It's odd." She rubbed her arms as if she were cold right

through her denim jacket. "Cemeteries have never bothered me before. But I feel all... I don't know. Uneasy."

"You can go back to the van if you—"

"No. No, I'm seeing this through. Look, there up ahead. Sousa."

There was a heavy mist in the air, droplets not heavy enough to fall as rain dampened their faces and clothes, but they hurried ahead to a large, gleaming black gravestone that resembled an upright, open book. The name SOUSA was engraved in all caps across the top, and there were three names underneath with dates of birth and dates of death. Three names.

Robert, Mindi, and Benji.

Maya reached out and touched the final date under Benji's name. "Twelve weeks," she whispered. "Only twelve weeks."

"There was another child," Johnny said.

"Another son," Jack added.

Maya shivered and looked around as the wind picked up a bit. "Let's get this done. She crouched and unzipped her bag, pulled out a hand spade, and handed it to Johnny. He took it and crouched beside her. "Right here?" He stabbed the spade into the ground."

"Yes, dead center."

"Bad pun," Jack said as she handed him two candles in glass jars. Then she pulled out a compass, and eyed the dial. "Put the black one there. The white one here," she pointed behind the grave and in front of it, then she placed two others to the left and right at the cardinal points. Johnny knew that because he noticed everything she did, and he'd seen her do magic a few times.

"Johnny, the contagious samples?" She held out a hand. He'd dug a small hole already, so he took the zipper bag from his pocket and gave it to her.

Maya took it and lay it in the hole, bag and all. "Johnny stand in the north. Jack, right here in the south." She placed them where she wanted them, then took two drawstring cotton pouches from her bag of tricks and handed one to each of them. The bag was weighty, as if it held sand. He tapped it against his palm and said, "What's in here?"

"Black tourmaline dust, ground bindweed, and blessed sea salt. Once they arrive, I'll signal you. When I do, Johnny start your bag of salt, making a circle from where you're are, to where Jack is standing, while Jack, you do the same, moving to where Johnny is standing. Overlap the starting points a little. It should seal them right here."

"Is that...cruel? Binding them here?" Jack asked.

"They get to choose. Stay here with their grave and whatever remains of their bodies, or move on. The only option we're taking away, is the one where they wreak havoc on the living."

Nodding, Johnny opened the drawstring bag and saw that Jack was doing the same. Maya knelt by the little hole, opened the zipper bag, and carefully took out the two gauze pads. She laid them side by side in the hole, and then tucked the bag into a pocket and still-kneeling, raised her arms up high. "Robert and Mindi Sousa," she said, her voice deep and powerful. "Come to your children." Rising, she began to move around the grave, slowly at first, then faster, chanting, "Hoof and horn, hoof and horn, you must die to be reborn. Corn and grain, corn and grain, all who die will rise again." Over and over she repeated the words in a cadence that grew faster and faster with her pace.

The wind blew harder. A few strands of Johnny's hair came loose from the band and whipped across his face. He swore the clouds moved over the sun in direct response to what Maya was doing, or maybe what her invited ghosts were doing.

She moved to the gravestone, arms up high, chanting even faster. The wind blew harder. No question it was working. None whatsoever. Maya's eyes were closed and her hair was twirling, caught as if in a twister. Jack's coat was plastered to his chest, the wind was blowing so hard. Another layer of darkness seemed to descend, and there was a groan, and then a snap, and the little cemetery gate came flying at them with deadly intent. Johnny lunged at Maya, tackling her flat to the ground just as the iron gate crashed into the headstone. He'd landed right on top of her, and for a moment she blinked right up into his eyes, and hers were wide.

Jack yelled, "Incoming!" from behind the large gravestone, and Johnny wrapped his arms around her and rolled them both, so they wound up with the stone protecting them, only this time she was on top of him, and feeling what he was feeling. For a second he was tempted to raise up his head and kiss her, but then Jack moved, reminding Johnny of his presence and the debris flying past them.

Maya got off him, and he got up onto his knees, and they huddled there behind the stone while the storm raged. A limb snapped off a nearby tree, and he saw three sections of the wrought iron fence do near-miss fly-bys.

"They can't get in," Jack said. "I think they can't get in. Look!"

All around the cemetery, darkness raged, a boundary of anger.

Maya lunged out from behind the stone, reaching around in front of it, and Johnny grabbed her around the waist and pulled her back.

She landed, leaned back on the headstone, tugged the zipper bag from her jeans pocket, opened her hand and dropped the two "contagious samples" in. Then she zipped it up.

A second ticked by, then two, and then it just stopped.

They lifted their heads, all of them, looking around. It grew lighter by degrees. The clouds moved away from the sun and the wind dropped to a chilly spring breeze.

Johnny sighed from the depths of his soul as they rose and moved out into the open again. "Okay. So that didn't work."

"But we learned a few things," Maya said. "There was another child."

"That has to be important," Johnny said. "But why couldn't the ghosts seem to get into the cemetary?"

MAGGIE SHAYNE

Jack was staring at something in the distance, and he said, "Maybe it has something to do with the dead. Or whatever has surrounded the place."

"What are you talking about, Jack?"

"I don't know." He lifted his phone and took a photo, like that was going to help.

Maya went to her black bag, pulled out a old school Polaroid, and pushed it into his hand. "I think you need actual film."

Jack took the camera, aimed and snapped, aimed and snapped, aimed and snapped. Photos were sliding out of the thing and into Maya's waiting hands. She handed some of them to Johnny. Jack was still shooting.

Johnny watched as the photographs developed and then he thought they couldn't be done, and then realized they were. Luminous white shapes, rather tall and slender, stood side by side just within the black iron cemetery fence.

Jack was still snapping, turning and snapping. "They go all the way around." Then he lowered the camera. "They're fading... wait, they're gone."

Johnny was picking up photos that had dropped from the camera to the ground. "Are they ghosts?"

"They can't be," Maya said. "We know the dead have to either move on, occupy a body, or move to the other side or they turn dark. They have to be something else."

"Like what?" Jack asked.

"Guardians of some kind?" She shrugged. "I don't know. But I think there are a lot more non-physical beings than physical ones. And everything physical has a non-physical version."

Johnny said, "Look, look at this."

He held up one of the photos. One of the slender shapes of light, was twisted midway up, as if to look back at them, and its face was a skull with wings and two crossed bones for a mouth.

"Death's head," Maya said softly. "It's not a puritan warning.

74

Someone must've seen them before, and started putting their faces on the graves."

Jack took the photo and looked at it. "So they were surrounding the graveyard, facing outward," Jack said. "Protecting this place."

"They're guardians," Johnny said. "We should leave an offering."

"I have some sandalwood in my bag," Maya said. "They'll like that."

CHAPTER TEN

*R*yan came downstairs around midday with bed-hair and a crooked smile. Kiley heard his feet pounding down the staircase a few minutes before he popped his head into the office. "Good morning, Ryan."

"Morning," he said. "Thanks a lot for letting us stay. I haven't slept like that in... ever."

"I'm glad to hear it." Kiley and Chris had been scouring the net for info and background on the parents, which he didn't need to see, so she clicked a random tab from her history, Ghosts in the Modern Age, and elbowed Chris to do likewise.

"Have they been bothering you that long?" she asked.

Ryan came up behind her and looked over her shoulder with interest. "Not so much bothering me. Not at first. They've been around as far back as I can remember."

"How did they interact with you in the beginning? What did they do?"

Ryan thought for a second, then said, "They'd soothe me back to sleep if I woke up at night. They went to school with me on my first day, so I wouldn't be scared. I knew nobody else could see them. I'd always known. I grew up with it, like learning to walk and talk. I just learned they were only for me."

"And… could you touch them? Physically?"

"I could kind of hold their hands, at first. It felt like holding cool mist or something. I'm not clear on when that started to change. After a while I couldn't touch them at all anymore. I could see them, hear them, sense when they were near. But not touch."

"They're not always near you?" Chris asked. He'd opened the case file and was keying in notes from Ryan's story.

"They're always nearby. Close, but not present. It's almost like they're in a closet waiting to jump out as needed." Ryan slid onto the vacant stool.

Chris looked at the kid with round eyes. "That's the scariest thing I've ever heard in my life."

"It was pretty scary for me, too." Ryan looked at Kiley and asked, "How did you do it, anyway? Ghost-proof this place?"

"It was mostly Maya. I assisted."

"So she's some kind of a…"

"She's a witch."

"A witch." He repeated it kind of like he wasn't sure what to make of the word. "And what's Johnny, a werewolf?"

"Don't be silly. Werewolves aren't real."

"I didn't used to think witches were real, either," Ryan said.

"Witchcraft is like…folk magic, you know."

"Magic and werewolves are in the same category to me. So, Maya's a witch. What are the rest of you?

"We aren't really sure," Kiley said. "I mean, Chris is a certifiable genius. That seems kinda supernatural to me. Johnny can apparently time travel."

"Wow."

"It's only happened once. Before that, all he could do was talk to the souls of people who were dying. And Jack, he can read people, and since he met me, he sees dead people on a pretty regular basis and sometimes they possess him and relive their trauma. So, I guess that makes him a channel?" She looked up at him. "How about you?"

He tucked in his chin. "What *about* me?"

"You see dead people."

"Only my parents."

"Are you sure?"

He frowned. "I never even thought of that. I mean, not, so far. But I haven't been looking, either."

"How do they look to you, your parents?" She noticed that Chris was getting everything down.

"Bad."

She frowned and looked at him. He wasn't looking back, though. He was looking inside himself, seeing, maybe, those ghosts. "Bad, how?"

"They used to look like normal people, only kind of …thin."

"Translucent?"

He shrugged.

"Like you can kind of see through them a little?"

"Yeah. Almost like they're being projected."

"You said they used to look normal?"

"Just like in the pictures of them my sister keeps all over the house, yeah." He lowered his eyes.

"So how do they look now?"

He pressed his lips. "It's almost like their bones are dissolving, except I guess they don't have bones. They're kind of sagging. Their eyes droop and their mouths hang way low at the corners, and their skin is turning darker and darker gray. They look like melting candles with their colors draining away."

"Jeeze," she said softly. "That's awful, Ryan. I'm so sorry."

He shrugged. "I don't know what made them change like that."

Chris said, "I think the part of them that was your parents fades with time, Ry. They're becoming just mindless rage-beings.

Like hurricanes, they're raw energy. Emotional energy, though, mostly anger and rage."

"Maya read us a passage from one of her books that said pretty much the same thing," Breia said softly. She had entered the room behind them with the breakfast she'd saved for her brother, reheated and steaming and smelling like it was time to eat again. "That makes more sense to me," she went on. "Our parents were kind and good."

Ryan got up, took the plate from his sister and looked at Kiley.

"You can eat in here, it's fine," she said before he could ask. She figured he was old enough not to dump syrup on her furniture.

He took the plate to the burgundy chair, and she second-guessed herself.

Then she turned to Breia. "We're making some notes. Is there anything you can tell us about your parents, especially details from around the time of their deaths?"

Breia started talking, and Chris sped up his key tapping pace. Kiley let her go on, and only interrupted to get details.

And then she saw a reflection in the window glass as someone passed by the open office door behind her, just walked right by. She was an ample woman in a skintight red dress and a pink feather boa. Her red hair was piled high and her makeup would've made a clown jealous. Kiley turned her head immediately, but the woman wasn't there. Yet she turned back to the window in time to see her reflection just as she moved out of sight, the smoke from her cigarette in its Cruella De Vil holder unfurling behind her, a carcinogenic ribbon.

And then she was gone.

Chris sneezed. He glanced at Ryan, then Kiley and Breia. "Did somebody sneak a smoke when I wasn't looking? Cause I'm allergic to that shit."

"You smell it?" Kiley asked.

"Don't you?" He sniffed the air. "They make flower scented e-cigs now?"

"Lilacs," Kiley said. "It smells like lilacs."

A sudden crashing sound came from outside. The lights brightened, then went out, and the computer screen turned black.

"What the hell was that?" Kiley went to the window to look out. Her mailbox was on her front porch, its post snapped off jaggedly at the bottom. She could see the broken bottom half of its post poking out of the ground in its rightful spot.

The wind was whipping up again.

"My parents are here," Ryan said. "And it looks like they're pissed."

A tree limb came flying at them, shattering the window as Kiley flung up her arms to shield her face.

"Holy mother of– Look out!"

She flung an arm around Ryan as more debris flew toward them, and brought him low to the floor with her, relieved to see Chris and Breia in a similar position nearby. Then, a street sign came winging in and its corner caught Breia in the forehead and knocked her flat on her back. And she didn't move.

"That's just about e-fucking-nough!" Kiley surged to her feet, lunging toward the window and screaming "GET OUT of MY HOUSE!" at the top of her voice. At the same instant, something kind of whooshed past her, or maybe through her from behind and out the front. It roared the same words Kiley shouted, at the same time she shouted them, and the wind cut off like a blown-out birthday candle. It didn't die down, it just *stopped*. The trash cans, branches and debris that had been flying toward the house, dropped to the ground outside as if someone had turned on the gravity.

Everybody stood up slowly except for Breia, who was still on the floor, eyes closed, bleeding from a gash in her forehead. Chris dashed into the bathroom and returned with a first aid kit to join Ryan, leaning over her.

Kiley pulled out the phone and dialed 911.

"We thought they wouldn't hurt us," Ryan said slowly. "No matter what else they might do, I was sure they would never hurt Breia or me." He shook his head, looking at Kiley. "How could they do this?" And then he looked toward the broken window with the tree limb hanging through it, half in, half out. "How could you do this? How could you hurt your own daughter? My sister! I hate you! I hate you, do you hear? I'll hate you forever!"

~

Johnny, Jack, and Maya stood where the cemetery gate had been, holding hands, their eyes closed. Maya began to hum a single note, and she squeezed Johnny's hand to tell him to hum too, so he did, and so did Jack. He stopped for a breath and started humming again, and after doing that a few times, he fell into a rhythm.

"Open your mind to hear, but don't focus on hearing," Maya said. "Focus on the breathing, on the humming. Let your awareness be open, but don't strain to hear. Allow. Relax. Attune to the light beings of this place."

Jack's phone pinged and he let go of Johnny's hand.

"*Jack!*" Maya said. Eyes open, circle broken.

"Sorry. Reflex." He slid the phone back without looking, rejoined hands, and they started over.

After a few minutes of the humming, Johnny felt oddly disconnected, like his head was floating far above his body. Not his head, he realized. His awareness.

"We offer thanks and we honor the guardians of this place." She lowered her head and her gaze to the little bowl of puffy white sage and ground, fragrant sandalwood she'd found in her bag.

A loud PING sounded, and once again, Jack released his hand. "Dammit, Jack."

"Something's wrong," Jack said. He looked at the phone, then turned it toward the other two so they could see Kiley's text.

Kiley: *Need you. Hurry.*

CHAPTER ELEVEN

"*B*etter take some pictures before you move the limb," Neighbor Rodney said to Kiley.

He'd come from his place across the street to stand in the yard beside her in his bathrobe, knee socks, and ankle high moccasin style slippers and offer unsolicited advice. It was as nice outside as if the ghost-storm had never happened. Then Rodney added, "I have a chainsaw. I can get that branch out of there for you."

Kiley swung her head around and up at him. Way up. Rodney was 6'4" with a build like a lumberjack. Not that she had ever seen a lumberjack, but it would explain the chainsaw.

"You would do that? That's really..." She searched for the word.

"Neighborly," he filled in for her. "Like I said, take pictures first. For the *in*surance." Accent on the "in." "Call me when you're ready. I'm off today, so I'll be home." Then he shook his head. "Freak storm, huh? A shame it messed up your sign."

"My sign?" And then she saw it, that beautiful sign she'd had made for the place, split in two on the front lawn with a cinder

85

block from who the hell knew where lying in between its broken sides. "Aw, *hell*, my sign!"

Jack's van pulled in. Johnny, Jack and Maya piled out and came running. "Is everybody okay?" Jack asked at the same time Maya said, "Whoa, what happened?"

They'd gathered on the front porch where Chris and Kiley had been picking up the broken glass that landed outside. Most had fallen inside.

"You okay?" Jack took Kiley by the shoulders, searching her face.

"Yeah, I'm okay." He hugged her close, one hand on her head and she felt like the most cherished being in the known universe. How mushy was that?

"Stop treating me like a fragile little girl child, McCain."

"Stop looking like one, Brigham," he said, but he said it smiling. Apparently, her state of shock was still visible on her face. "So, what happened?"

"It was the ghosts. They attacked. Started hurling stuff at the house. Put that tree limb through the window. Hit Breia in the head with a street sign."

"Is she okay?" Johnny asked.

"She just needed a few stitches, the EMT said. Ambulance took her to the ER, but she was with it enough to forbid any of us going with her. Said she wanted us here, protecting Ryan."

"Screw that," Johnny said. "She shouldn't be alone with all this going on. I'm going."

"Johnny's right," Maya said. "They attacked us the same way at the cemetery. But Breia's injury changes our calculus. They're willing to hurt their own kids. That's a whole different level of bad."

Jack nodded. "Are we sure it was them? Did anyone see them?"

"Ryan did," Kiley said.

"Where's Ryan now?"

"Picking up the glass in the office," she replied. "But maybe he shouldn't be alone. Chris..."

"I'll go." Chris fist-bumped Johnny and they headed in opposite directions, Chris into the house, and Johnny to his truck.

Maya watched him get in, and kept watching until he'd driven around the corner and out of sight. Then she turned back toward Kiley, who pretended she hadn't noticed her longing gaze. "I'd better get busy re-setting the wards and powering up the circle," she said. "I'll reinforce it at sunrise and sunset from now on." She walked away and Kiley wondered if it would be enough.

She turned to Jack, took a breath and said, "I think there's something in the house."

"You said they didn't get in," he reminded her.

"They broke through, and I'm pretty sure they were coming in. Then something..."

"Something..." He nodded at her to go on, his attention fully on what she was saying.

"It came from behind me, whooshed past me. Not past me, through me." She shivered and rubbed her arms. "It emitted this primal yell that chilled me to the bone but it said exactly what I said while I was saying it."

"Which was."

"Get the fuck out of my house, or something to that effect." She shrugged. "And then they were just...gone."

"The parental ghosts?"

"Yeah. It was like she blew them out."

"Like who blew them out?" She shook her head and he said "Hey." He looked into her eyes. "I'm here. You can talk to me."

She nodded. "I know."

"Did you hear the voice aloud?"

"No, it was more like I felt it."

"Huh." He frowned. "Did the others...?"

"They knew *something* had happened, but not what. You think I'm going woo-woo?"

"I don't know. Has there been anything else?"

She nodded. "A woman laughing. And sometimes making smart-ass comments. And just before the attack today, I thought I saw her reflection in the window glass. She walked right past the office doorway, smoking a cigarette." Then she snapped her fingers. "Chris smelled the smoke. It made him sneeze. And it smelled like lilacs!"

"Who is she?"

"I don't know."

"Huh." Then he looked past her, and his eyes rounded a little. "I don't want to alarm you, hon, but Rodney from across the street is heading this way with a chainsaw."

She laughed in spite of everything. Nobody could tease her out of a dark moment like Jack. He was very good, her man. "He said he'd get the tree out of the window for us."

"Wow, really? That's so neighborly of him. Hey, we'd better take some pictures first."

Chris came outside looking around the yard, clearly alarmed. "I can't find Ryan anywhere," he said before they could ask what was wrong. "He must've gone after Breia."

Johnny got to the ER just as Breia was being led to the exit by a nurse. Her head was already bandaged, and she looked like she was okay.

"Breia." He said it and sighed his relief at the same time.

"I told everyone not to come," she said. "It's not safe anywhere else."

"They broke through Maya's barricades. I don't see that it matters, now."

"No," she said. "They didn't get inside. Something stopped them."

He nodded, not surprised. Maya had skills. His admiration for her, warm and familiar and ever-present, glowed a little brighter. But he ought to be focused on Breia. She was the one in the ER, after all. "Are you all right?"

Breia nodded. "Where's Ryan?"

The nurse handed her some papers and walked away. "He's at the house. It's quiet now, or was when I left." Johnny slid his arm through hers and led her through the doors into the parking lot.

He looked at her head. "How bad?"

"Seven stitches and an X-ray. I'm fine."

"It must hurt."

"A lot," she said.

"They give you anything?" He opened the passenger door of his truck and helped her up.

"Yes. It's kicking in, but…"

"But what?"

She didn't answer, just settled into her seat and closed the truck door.

Johnny went around to get in his side and started driving them back to toward Kiley's. He had to tell her what he'd found out at the cemetery. That she'd had another brother. But she still seemed pretty shaken up.

Breia said, "It's not just physical. The pain."

"I can imagine."

"I think my own parents just tried to kill me," she said. He could hear her tears through the cracks in her voice. "I can't believe it."

"It wasn't them, Breia." He covered her hand with one of his, glancing sideways at her on and off while he drove. "It wasn't them."

"It wasn't *not* them."

He was trying to explore the depth of that statement, when his phone went off and hers did, too.

She picked hers up first, since he was driving. "Oh, shit. Kiley says Ryan's gone. He slipped out while they were cleaning up."

Johnny pulled the truck over, checked that traffic was clear, and made a U-turn in the street. "We should check the hospital. That's probably where he's going."

"I'm texting him now. Where are you, Ryan?" she asked as she typed. "You'd better freaking answer me. I'm so sick of you pulling these vanishing acts all the time."

She watched her phone, but he didn't respond.

"Fine. I'll use the app." She tapped the phone again, then sat back in the seat staring at the device in disbelief. "'Find My Phone has been disabled on the device you're attempting to locate.'" Johnny realized she was reading the error message from the screen. "Ryan, I'm going to kill you and save our parents the trouble." She typed as she said it, thumbs hammering the poor phone as if punishing it for a crime.

Then she tapped the speaker button and he heard ringing on the other end.

"Urgent Care, can you hold?"

"No I can't. I'm looking for a missing seventeen-year-old boy who would've been there in the last thirty minutes."

"Yes, he was looking for his sister who'd just been released. Only missed her by a little while."

"Did he say where he was going?"

"No, I'm sorry."

"Thank you." She disconnected and turned to Johnny, searching his eyes as if he had the answers. Then she said, "Home. He must've gone home. Where else would he go?"

"Let's go find out."

Breia kept looking at him as he drove. Johnny would glance back and catch her. Finally, she said, "I'm sorry, I just can't believe how much you're helping me, us, right now. I keep thinking it's some kind of miracle."

"I... It's what we do."

"I feel like this is above and beyond, Johnny," she said, and she reached across the distance between them and slid her hand over his on the steering wheel. "Am I wrong?"

"I'm... um... Oh, shit, was that the turn?" He braked a little too hard and she took her hand away to brace herself on the seat. Johnny felt something in his chest that might've been panic.

"No, it's fine. You can take the next one." She relaxed into her seat and stopped telling him how great he was for the rest of the drive.

CHAPTER TWELVE

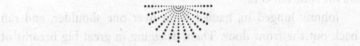

*W*hen Johnny pulled into the driveway of the pretty white house, a shiver whispered over his nape and he reached behind him to rub the spot. Nothing looked off.

"It was our parents' house," Breia said. "We inherited it when they died." She did not get out of the truck. "Do you think they're here?"

"If they're going to be anywhere, seems like they'd be here," Johnny said. "You should stay in the truck. I'll go in."

"That's sweet of you, but no." She opened the pickup door and got out. As soon as she set one foot on the pavement, Johnny thought the wind picked up. Leaves skipped across the bare lawn, clung for a moment to old blades of last year's grass before being swept away again. A leaf didn't stand a chance against the wind, did it?

He got out his side and hurried around to hers, watching all around them as he walked her along the flagstone path. The green shoots peering out through year-old mulch in the flowerbeds were taller than before. Three concrete steps led up to the door beneath a miniature of the house's pointed roof.

She turned the knob and said, "It's unlocked," as she pushed the door open. And then as they walked in, "Do you smell that?"

"It's gas. Stay outside! Don't breathe this shit." Johnny pulled his coat over his face and ran inside, ducking into the living room on pure intuition. It was an inherent sense. You experienced it, you didn't question it. He felt the kid. There he was, right there on the sofa, out cold.

Johnny lunged in, hauled Ryan over one shoulder, and ran back out the front door. Then, dragging in great big breaths of air on purpose, he kept running across the lawn, away from the place in case it blew.

He laid Ryan on the grass, leaning close to feel for a pulse and finding one. Then he lifted his gaze and looked around. "Breia! Where are you?"

"Coming!" She came out the front door of the house, and he swore under his breath as she came running and fell to her knees beside her brother. She was coughing and breathing way too fast. "Is he–?"

"He's breathing," Johnny said. "I called 911. Why did you go in there? That place could've blown up with you inside. One spark–"

"That place is all we have. The burners were on in the kitchen. I turned them off, opened some windows and ran right back out here."

Ryan started to cough.

Breia stared at him, her eyes welling. "Ryan," she cried, pressing his face between her palms. "Ryan, baby. I know you've been through hell, but you can't give up now. Not now, when we finally have someone to help us."

He squeezed his entire face up, then slowly blinked his vision into focus. "Let me up," Ryan said as he tried to rise.

Johnny helped him into a sitting position. He looked around. "I couldn't get out," he said. He was breathing really hard and fast. "They locked me in. They tried to gas me."

As he spoke, he clasped Johnny's forearms to hold himself upright, and Johnny felt that sensation of falling again.

Johnny blipped back in time, but apparently, only a little while back. He knew the feeling now, so he wasn't confused about what was happening. He was standing outside the hospital when Ryan got out of an Uber at the ER.

Nobody had seen Johnny so far, and he kept out of sight, so no one would. He thought he should probably do his best to go unseen when he time-hopped.

Ryan sighed as he came back out the double doors. Johnny knew he'd just learned that he'd missed his sister. The kid's Uber was long gone, but he looked around and spotted a solution. There was one of those rental bikes on the corner and his house wasn't far.

Johnny wondered if the parents were tired out from their latest rage storm. Maybe they needed to rest between cycles. He hoped so, because the kid was unprotected and out in the open.

Ryan swiped his card and took the bike, then pedaled away like some normal kid without a care in the world.

Johnny started to jog after him, assuming there was something here he was supposed to see. But as soon as he started to run, he found himself on the front lawn of the Sousa place. "Whoa."

Ryan pedaled into the front yard, jumped off and let the bike keep going until it tipped over on its own as he walked away. Johnny stepped behind a tree, but the kid never even looked in his direction.

He used his key, went inside, and just as Johnny lunged out to shout a warning, the door slammed. Ryan was pounding on the door from the other side and yelling, "What the hell? What the actual *hell*? Are you going to kill me now?"

"Jeeze, I feel drunk," Ryan said.

Johnny was once again kneeling on the ground beside the kid in the exact spot he'd been before. He wondered if Breia had noticed him blip out for a second, but since she wasn't reacting to it, he didn't think so.

"I swear to God, I was not trying to kill myself, Breia. It was them. The place was full of gas when I got here. They locked the door, knocked me over the head—"

"And put him on the sofa," Johnny said. "I believe you, Ryan." He met Breia's eyes, nodded once. "It's the truth."

Breia snapped her arms around Ryan's neck, hugging and whispering, "Thank God!"

"Thank God our parents tried to murder me just now?" he asked, but he hugged her back.

"Thank God it wasn't you." She wiped at her eyes. "You've been so depressed. I didn't even realize how much, until I saw the change in you at Kiley's house. It was like a dark cloud had lifted."

"Because it had," Johnny said. "And it will again once we get you back to the house. That's our goal for right now, okay?" He tried to sound confident and sure of himself, when inside he wondered if the gang from Spook Central had met its match. These ghosts were powerful. And furious.

A siren wailed nearer as an ambulance pulled up alongside the road.

Johnny moved a few steps away and placed a video call to headquarters. Maya answered from the computer bar in the office. He could see off to her side that the tree limb was gone. So were the curtains. There was cardboard duct-taped over the big sunny window in the library.

"What is that?" Maya asked. "Is that an ambulance behind you?"

He realized he'd been pacing with the phone. "Yeah, everyone's okay. I think. We found Ryan out cold in his house with the gas turned on. His parents locked him in, tried to kill him."

"Holy shit. Is he okay?"

"I think so. EMTs are giving him the once over." He turned the phone to show her. Ryan was behind an oxygen mask, with an EMT and Breia both crouching nearby.

"You need to get him back here as soon as he gets the medical all-clear, Johnny. This is the only place he's safe."

"But he wasn't even safe there."

"Yes, he was," Maya insisted. "They didn't get in here. I mean, it was close, and they did some damage. They were even able throw things at us, but they could not get in. Just like at the cemetery."

"That's what Breia said, too. Your wards are that good?"

"No," Maya said. "They're not. That assault was way too powerful for my skill level. But all the same, they didn't get in here."

She was saying something without really saying it. And he remembered Ryan's feeling that *something* was in the house. It sounded like one of those topics he and Maya could dissect for hours. He guessed they didn't do that anymore. No, he thought. They didn't do that right now. But maybe they would again.

"We need you back here, Johnny."

"I'm on my way. Just as soon as I can."

"Be careful. These things…they're powerful. And angry. I've never felt such anger."

"I know. I feel it, too."

"We're changing, you know," she said. "Working together, I think it's somehow enhancing all our abilities. I mean, I couldn't slam a door from a distance before. And your power has changed, too. And I think something's up with Kiley. We need to discuss this, all of us together. But first we just need you here, safe. Okay?"

"Okay. I'll see you soon," he said, and it came out kind of raspy and dumb. He ended the call, pocketed the phone. Ryan was still holding an oxygen mask to his face, and the medic crouched nearby, speaking to him, her eyes sharp and observant. Breia's focus was riveted to her brother. Around them, nothing seemed unusual, but all the same, that chill on the back of Johnny's neck remained.

He saw the EMT packing up his kit and returned to Ryan, who was getting up onto his feet again with Breia's help.

"He's okay," she said. "We can have him check in with a doctor if there are any symptoms."

"Thank God," Johnny said, and he clapped Ryan's shoulder. "You sure you feel okay?"

"Yeah, yeah, I'm good."

"And what about the house?" he asked Breia.

She nodded toward the open door. Fire fighters were going in and out. "I'm leaving them a key so they can lock up when they finish here," she said.

"I think we should get you both back to Kiley's, then. It's clearly not safe anywhere else."

"Wait," Ryan said. "Why are we not discussing the fact that my parents just tried to gas me? After splitting my sister's head open, which could've killed her?" Ryan's face was lax with shock as he seemed to digest the enormity of it all, now that he'd survived the attempt.

"Why are they doing this?"

Johnny felt the blip coming and moved two steps from their line of sight just before he fell into the past.

There was a little boy riding his bicycle across an all but empty parking lot. In the distance, teenage Breia was clapping her hands and whooping as the little guy sped, wobbling dangerously and yelling, "I'm doing it! I'm doing it!" He was curving directly toward the road, though, and panic came over his face and he said, "I can't steer! Help, I can't stop!"

Breia lunged toward him with superhuman speed, but she

wasn't fast enough. Ryan didn't have control and a car was speeding nearer. There was no question the two were going to collide, but then, just as Ryan wobbled into the road screaming, the car veered to the right and hit a pole. Just drove right into it. *Crunch.*

Breia reached Ryan, who had wiped out and lay on the pavement crying. She carried him and his bike out of the road and headed for the safe area nearby.

Johnny threw up a stop sign hand and said, "Wait, wait," and time froze. It was so surreal he had to take a breath and close his eyes to get his bearings. There was a small dandelion seed, fluffy and floating right in front of his face. It just hung there, motionless, suspended. He saw a butterfly, a bee, a person on a pogo stick a block away, not quite touching the sidewalk.

He moved his hand from right to left, and time reversed. Or that's what it felt like. He stopped moving his hand just before Ryan reached the spot where parking lot spilled onto busy road. "Okay, now, slowly..." He moved his hand very slowly right, and time crept forward in ultra slow-mo. Ryan and his bike moved inch by inch into the path of the car, which was closer to him with every frame. Then there was something, a distortion between the car and the kid, a shape. But not one made of light, like the forms in the Polaroid shots Jack had taken at the cemetery. This was a misshapen blob of light gray.

This time, Johhny was right on top of it as it happened. Ryan's bike went over sideways as he panicked and Johnny reached for the kid by sheer instinct. His hand skimmed Ryan's shoulder. For just an instant, Johnny felt the road skinning Ryan's knee right through his jeans and the terror of what was coming next, as if both were happening to him. He looked up and saw a man and a woman standing there in the road right between him and the car. The woman screamed and swung her arms in a right to left arc, and the car moved in the exact same motion, swinging suddenly sideways and right into the pole. And then the two of them returned to Ryan, leaning over him.

It's okay, we won't let anything hurt you, you're safe. They said the things parents say to comfort terrified children. They were not scary looking. Kind of translucent and gray, but otherwise, they resembled the photos he'd spotted inside the house, except that they looked tired, or maybe hungover.

Then Breia put her hands on Ryan, and Johnny blipped back into the present. He took stock of where he was and who could see him. He was near his truck, partially hidden by its nose. The EMTs were still packing up.

"You okay, Johnny?" Breia asked.

He nodded, but he couldn't stop looking at Ryan. He didn't look the way he'd looked before. He looked way more shaken and terrified. And no wonder.

Up until recently, he'd had a pair of soggy looking guardian angels watching over him. Now, apparently, they were trying to kill him.

CHAPTER THIRTEEN

hen the house was aired out sufficiently, Ryan and Breia were allowed back inside to pick up a few things. Johnny didn't like it, but he felt like there was a pattern. The ghosts were always quiet for a while between incidents. He estimated they would still have time to get back to Spook Central safely before they had the energy to try again.

While he was waiting for Breia and Ryan, he got a call he didn't expect. The return number was simply POLICE.

It made his heart jump a little as he picked up. "Hello?"

"It's Lieutenant Mendosa," she said. He'd have recognized her voice. "Listen, um, I had the local PD do a wellness check on your grandfather at that address you gave me."

"And?" He waited, almost holding his breath.

"A retired couple live there. Say they know him, but haven't seen him in years. They have no idea why he would say he was going there."

He frowned hard, not comprehending.

"Listen, do you want me to open a missing persons case? He's old. Nobody knows where he is. And he's gone silent for what, four days now?"

"Almost," Johnny said. "And yes, I think that missing persons thing is a good idea. I mean, I guess." Then again, he didn't know his grandfather. Had barely spent any time at all with him before he'd up and left. Surely someone would know if something had happened to him? But would anyone notify Johnny? Had his grandfather even told anyone he existed?

"Okay, I'll do it."

"We're ready." Breia came down the stairs, a wheeled suitcase thumping behind her. She came over to him at the door, and smiled up into his eyes.

Johnny said, "Thank you, Lieutenant. I appreciate the help."

"*De nada*," she replied and disconnected.

He pocketed his phone. Breia said, "You've become... our hero, I guess."

"Yeah, don't thank me until we've solved the problem." Speaking of which, do you have anything of your parents'?"

She paused, frowning. "There's a whole box of stuff in the garage. Maybe two. There were some things I just couldn't get rid of, but couldn't have around the house either, you know?"

"Can we bring them along?"

"We can grab them on the way out. Gosh, it's been years. Ryan had just started to walk when I packed it all away."

Ryan came thundering down the stairs with a bulging backpack over his shoulder and a computer bag in hand.

"What, we don't have enough computers for you?" Johnny asked.

His eyes were still kind of hollow, probably still in shock from having his parents try to kill him. Not to mention the after effects of propane inhalation. "My gaming laptop. Chris said he'd tweak it out for me."

"Is that a technical term?" Breia asked, taking Johnny's cue to try and lighten the mood.

Ryan gave a token smile and nodded, and then they went out

to the truck. With everyone inside and their bags stowed in the back, Johnny backed up to the garage door and got out to open it. Then he backed right inside next to Breia's little car.

It occurred to him that she might want her car with her, but he decided not to suggest it in case the ghosts caused trouble. He kept getting chills up his spine as Breia moved aside a few boxes to find the ones she wanted while Ryan sat in the truck, motionless, earbuds in place.

"Here they are. Three boxes. More than I thought."

"Let me, let me." He took the box she'd pulled out and set it in the back of the truck, then turned and she handed him another. She brought the third box and leaned over the truck to put it in. "That's it." She looked around. "And no murder attempts. Nice."

"So far, so good." He walked her right up to the passenger door, feeling like an anvil was going to fall from the sky at any moment. She got in, and he closed her door and hurried around to his side. He kept getting chills and his nerves were jumping. The air was electric, like during a lightning storm. As far as he was concerned, the faster they were back at Spook Central, the better.

Kiley sat in the office, in the sitting area she loved, with a cup of tea. Maya had brewed a full pot of this minty herbal blend she said had calming and healing properties and would help them all recover from the trauma of the attack.

Jack was outside with the contractor who was replacing the window glass. The frame was undamaged and original to the house, so he was replacing the large pane of glass.

Chris was at the computer bar, researching Robert and Mindi Sousa. Every now and then he would shout out an interesting tidbit. "Robert's grandparents immigrated from Greece all the way back in the forties." Or "Mindi worked for Future-Tech in New York. Quit the year Breia was born."

She sipped her tea and waited for the calm to happen.

Maya's phone buzzed. She said, "It's Johnny," then put it on speaker and set the phone on the coffee table.

"We thought you'd be back by now," she said. "Everything all right?"

Chris came over to the sitting area so he could hear better.

"We're on our way," Johnny said. "We got some of the parents' personal things."

"That's a really good idea," Maya said.

"Um, listen, Lieutenant Mendosa called. My grandfather isn't in Florida. His friends there say he never was. So she's getting a missing persons case going."

"*What!*" Kiley's explosive word was not a question. "Johnny, do you think something's happened to him? My God…"

"You all probably know him better than I do. Maybe he just wanted some space."

"That's not it, Johnny," Maya said. "He was out of his mind happy you found him, and so proud. He told me so."

Jack heard it as he came through the French doors into the room and moved closer to the phone. "He told me the same," Jack said. "We'll find him, rookie. Don't worry. In case you haven't noticed, we're kind of a good team."

"We are."

"We'll watch for you," Maya said. "Be careful, Johnny. This has escalated in a very dark way."

"Yeah. If we'd have been a few minutes later finding Ryan… Anyway, we're heading back now."

Jack said. "What's your ETA?"

"Ten minutes."

"Good. Sooner the better. See you then."

The call ended. Maya tapped the phone. "Something has changed," she said, looking at the others. "Up to now, these two have been trying to protect Ryan. Now they're trying to kill him. What happened to Breia might have been unintentional, but locking Ryan in the house and cranking on the gas was no accident. What's different?"

"We are," Chris said. "We're getting in their way. Getting in between them and their kids."

"Yeah, and we aren't the only ones." Everyone looked at Kiley. She took a breath and took another sip of tea.

"Something chased those ghosts out of here," Chris said. "They got past Maya's wards and threw a tree at us, hit Breia in the head with a street sign, and would've done worse, but something stopped them. And I really want to know what it was. I just...felt it. Like a shock wave from a distant blast."

"That's good, that's good, that's how it felt to me, too," Kiley said. "And it shouted like a thousand tone-deaf hell demons."

Tone deaf? How dare you!

She frowned and looked at them all. "Okay, so, did no one else hear that?"

Chris and Maya exchanged a look. Jack nodded at Kiley. "What did she say this time?"

"She was offended by the tone deaf part. Not the demon part, mind you."

"She?" Chris asked. "She, who?"

"You know how you smelled cigarette smoke earlier, Chris?" Kiley asked.

He nodded. "Lilac scented tobacco, yes."

"I thought I saw a woman move past the doorway," she pointed as she spoke. "Big red hair, slinky dress, cigarette in a long holder. And then you smelled the smoke."

He nodded, looked around and said, "I'm allergic," in a really loud voice.

"And when we were painting the porch, Maya," Kiley rushed on, "and you said no ghost could get in, I heard her laughing."

"Holy shit. A house ghost? We have a house ghost?" Maya

seemed weirdly excited about the prospect, which made Kiley want to smack her.

"Is that a thing?" she asked.

Maya shrugged. "Apparently. And you felt like it was this house ghost who chased the parental-ghosts away?"

"It makes perfect sense," Jack said. "They couldn't come into the cemetery because they can't go where ghosts are."

"Where non-physical beings are," Maya said. "I don't think those cemetery dwellers were ghosts."

"I was furious," Kiley said. "I sort of let my temper blast out, you know? I leaned toward the window yelled at the ghosts to get out of my house, and when I did, it felt like something else yelled it, too. Like it joined in and made me bigger, louder, and we sort of roared together. And then they were gone."

"I feel entirely left out," Jack said. "I'm the guy who talks to dead people."

Kiley shrugged. "Sorry to walk on your lawn, but it is what it is."

"Well," Maya said, "At least she's on our side. Whoever she is." She looked around the room up high, as one does. "I guess the polite thing would be to thank her."

"Yeah," Kiley said, and she got up from the sofa and said, "Thank you," expressively spreading her arms. "You might have saved our lives and we're grateful. If there's anything we can do for you in return, we'd be more than – " *BANG.* "What the hell?"

A large framed print that had been on the wall was now on the floor with a crack across its glass. It had been Chris's contribution to their office decor. *Dogs Playing Poker.*

"Everybody's a critic," Chris said.

A vehicle approached and gave a beep-beep. "That's Johnny." Maya rushed to the front door. Everyone spilled out onto the porch, and Kiley waved as the pickup came closer, and then suddenly, the whole world started to shake.

A wave moved beneath her feet, lifting the porch up and

down, and Kiley grabbed the railing with one hand and Jack with the other.

"Earthquake!" Chris said, moving into the doorway and bracing his hands on the frame while Maya clung to the railing at the top of the porch steps.

CHAPTER FOURTEEN

Johnny saw the gang gathering on the front porch as he drove nearer. Maya stood on the top of the steps, her sunshine hair dancing in the spring breeze, her smile welcoming him back. Suddenly, she grabbed hold of the railing and held on as if for dear life.

For a moment he was confused. Then he felt the shaking underneath him. The road buckled and rose up in front of the truck. "Everybody hold on!" He jerked the wheel left, hard, veering off the road, into the ditch and clung to the steering wheel to hold himself behind it. Breia pressed one hand to the ceiling and gripped the "oh-shit-handle" above the passenger door as Johnny kept the pedal down. The powerful motor carried the truck right through the ditch and out the other side, past the macadam barricade and back onto the pavement beyond as its passengers bounded up and down on its seats. He aimed for Kiley's driveway and stomped it, but the ground was shaking under him still harder. He was almost there when a utility pole crashed right in front of him and he hit the brakes, leaving rubber on the pavement. Wires snapped in two, whipping and spitting sparks like electric cobras.

He looked around, spotted a gap and gunned it again. The truck lurched forward, veered left around one snapping power line, then over the top of the fallen pole, and then sharply right to avoid another live wire, and finally came to a stop on the front lawn.

"Inside, fast! Leave everything!"

Breia and Ryan dove out of the truck, scrambling for the front steps, only to fall as soon as they started to climb them, the shaking was so intense.

Johnny came behind, bracing them both, and Maya reached down from the top stair. Her other arm was wrapped around the post there. She clasped Ryan's hand and pulled, and Ryan kept his arm around his sister. In that moment he seemed like a full-on man, determined, strong, and furious. He pulled Breia up with him. She was shaking and unsteady.

The minute Breia and Ryan were on the porch itself, the shaking stopped.

"Son of a …" Kiley picked herself up off the porch floor. Jack gave her a hand and asked if she was okay, but she didn't answer. Instead, she shook her fist and shouted at the sky. "What the fuck is wrong with you? What kind of parents are you, anyway?"

Jack put his hands on her shoulders and said "Neighbors, sweetie."

Said neighbors were emerging like recently frightened woodland creatures, stunned and shaken. They stood on their lawns, all up and down the road, probably wondering why the nice lady who lived where bodies had been buried, was shouting at something only she could see.

Kiley smiled at them, gave a finger wave and said, "Freakin' earthquakes, anyway, am I right?"

They gathered in the dining room kind of automatically and Johnny thought he knew why. It was in the middle of the house, no windows, no outer walls. The office had too much glass, with its French doors and windows, one of them brand new, on that rear wall. Usually, he loved the view from that room and the way the sun had poured in all winter long. Now, not so much.

"What did I miss?" Johnny asked.

Jack had just come from the kitchen with a box of store bought chocolate chip cookies and bottle of chilled wine. Juice for Ryan. "Apparently we have a house ghost," he said.

Maya had already filled him in. And she was looking at him now, expectantly. No one had yet told Breia and Ryan about their deceased sibling, what with the attack, Briea's trip to the ER and the attempt on Ryan's life. And it was time, he knew that.

Chris had his laptop out. Maya sat surrounded by stacks of books from their ever-expanding reference library. Just last week Jack had scored what purported to be the original Book of Shadows of the Stregha, Maddalena. Folklorist and author Charles Godfrey Leland had published *Aradia or the Gospel of the Witches* in 1889, claiming Maddalena's manuscript as its source material. Many disputed such a manuscript ever existed. Yet here it was, on the Spook Central dining room table.

Jack and Kiley were also skimming books, one after another. They would read silently for long minutes, then read a quote of interest aloud, each one a potential clue. Just then, Kiley piped up with, "'Places of the dead are hallowed ground. No priest nor holy man need bless it to make it so. No evil may dwell where the dead rest.'"

"That would explain what we saw at the cemetery," Jack said. The photos were on the table too. They'd passed them around.

Breia said, "I wish you'd grabbed a shot of our parents' grave. I'd have liked to have seen it. It's been so long I don't remember." She and Maya stood at the end of the table nearest the living room, going through the boxes from Briea's garage. Her parents' possessions occupied the floor and chairs near them. "I supposed I could drive out there. I just...I don't know, I feel kind of scared of that place."

He had to tell her. Both of them.

"It's so quiet out there," Breia said with a look toward the front of the house. Her eyes were still wide and wary. Johnny's heart twisted in his chest to see how scared she was. "It's almost worse than when they rage."

"That makes sense, though," Kiley said. She flipped back a page in the book she'd been perusing. "Here it is. 'Woe to those souls which, failing to cross through the Veil at the moment of their demise, for the anguish of being unmoored from the body and adrift between the worlds is an agony beyond human imagining. The longer the soul remains unmoored, the greater this pain becomes. There are some who equate it to the suffering of those in hell, and some who believe it to be one and the same. The endless pain cannot be contained, and so it becomes rage, and the rage becomes a fierce power that can wreak havoc upon the human world. When a burst of such fury is spent, those tormented soul are as wraiths, thin and weak until their pain causes the power to build again. The older the ghost, the greater the pain of separation, the bigger the rages become.'" She lifted her eyes from the book to look at each of them.

Ryan was the only one who didn't return her steady gaze. He was playing a game on his cell phone, earbuds in, the momentary manliness he'd displayed in shielding his sister earlier, on a temporary hold.

"So, they'll be back for more," Breia said. "As soon as they're done resting." She was holding a framed photo in her hands. Her parents' wedding photo, white gown, black tux, adoring smiles, red and white roses. They'd been good people. Johnny had to keep reminding himself of that.

He glanced at Ryan, sitting right across from him. "How are you holding up?"

Ryan removed one earbud. "Sorry?"

"I asked how you're holding up."

He tapped his phone with a thumb, pausing whatever was in progress there. "I'm scared," he said. "I don't like to admit it, but I am. You know always before, they were protecting me. Now they're trying to kill me."

"I wonder if they're even in control of it," Kiley said. "This book reads as if the pain builds up until it releases in a burst of violence. Almost as if it becomes an entity of its own, or takes them over."

"We're going to stop them," Johnny said.

"Yeah? How?" Ryan looked around the place. "We can't stay here forever and you saw what they can do. Every attack is worse than the one before."

"I can put wards around your house, just like I did here," Maya said. She had a teddy bear in her hands that had been in one of the boxes. It was old and faded and hung heavily as if wet or weighted. Breia was looking at it with a puzzled frown.

"And then what?" Ryan asked. "I stay in my house for the rest of my life? I don't go to school? I don't drive? I don't date?" He shook his head and muttered, "Might as well let them take me," under his breath. Johnny didn't think anyone else heard.

The kid was still traumatized. Could he handle any more? Like learning he had a dead brother?

"There's a solution," Jack said. "Let's think about this. We've done this a few times. And every time it comes down to figuring out what the hell the ghost wants. So, what do they want?"

"To kill us." Ryan plugged his earbud back in and leaned back in his chair.

Johnny reached across and plucked the buds out. "Why do they want you dead?"

"I don't know. Because they've turned into freaking mindless demons or something?"

"No," Breia said. "They've only become violent toward us since you all have been helping us."

Ryan frowned and nodded, sitting up straighter and putting his phone down. "True. This is the first time they couldn't be right up in my face," Ryan said. "I've tried everything. Churches. Graveyards. I even bought some bullshit anti-ghost crystals at one of those lame tourist shops in the village."

Jack snapped his fingers. "*That's* where I've seen you before."

"So... all this is just because they want to be with Ryan?" Breia asked.

"And we've been preventing it," Maya said. "Which is making them angrier—"

"Which is making them stronger." Johnny closed his eyes and lowered his head. "There was something else at the cemetery, something you need to know."

Maya dropped the teddy bear on the table and reached for the next item in the box. But the teddy bear clunked when it hit, and she turned back around. "Breia, I think there's something inside your bear."

"That's not my bear. I don't know whose it is."

She reached for the bear, then stopped with her hand above it and sent her brother a wide-eyed look. It felt as if she might be afraid of the thing.

Ryan got up, went to the end of the table, and picked up the bear. He held up the paw, where a name was embroidered in fraying thread. "Who is Benji?"

"I don't know anyone named Benji." Breia looked at her brother.

"Neither do I. That thing looks old."

Johnny sighed, and said, "Yeah, that's what I wanted to talk to you about." He took out the pocket knife he'd been carrying around with him since his grandfather had run off. Its handle was onyx and inlaid with turquoise and citrine. He only knew what the stones were because Maya had told him. Gramp had left it behind and Johnny thought it must've been a mistake. The knife was special, and precious to him. He handed it to Ryan.

And then he talked while Ryan opened the bear along a seam to see what was inside.

"There was another Sousa buried with your parents," Johnny said. "Benji Sousa. Apparently, he was your brother."

"What?" Breia looked from Johnny to Ryan, who opened the bear, closed the knife, and handed it back to him.

"I might have something here," Chris said. He was on Ryan's side of the table, tapping keys on a laptop.

Ryan reached into the bear to pull out a square wooden box painted white, with a rose on its lid.

"What...what is it?" Breia asked. She leaned closer. Ryan handed her the box, but she backed away.

"For crying out loud, Breia." Ryan pulled it back, opened it up and looked inside. "It's a baby. Benji, I presume?"

He took out a photo framed between two oval panes of glass with beveled edges. The image was of an impossibly small, wrinkled newborn with a cap of dark hair and tightly closed eyes. The infant was so small it seemed like a fairy-child rather than a human one. He passed the photo to Breia, who gazed at it for long seconds until Johnny noticed the reverse and told her, "There's printing on the back."

She flipped it over and read aloud. "'Benji Sousa. Born... wait. That's two years after me. Died... twenty days later."

"Got it!" Chris said. "'Bennett Marcus Sousa was born prematurely and died in a neonatal ICU," Chris said. He spun his laptop around so they could see its screen. "There was a memorial service for him. There's an obituary."

Breia came to lean closer, and read aloud from the screen. "'Our precious Benji, firstborn son, was delivered at barely twenty weeks of life and lived only three more here in this world. He leaves behind an older sister, Breia, and two devastated parents, Robert and Mindi.'"

MAGGIE SHAYNE

She lifted her eyes to meet Ryan's. "We had a baby brother."

"*You* had a baby brother. I wasn't even born yet." Ryan lifted his eyes and looked around, suddenly nervous. "They're furious. I can feel it. They're out of their minds that they can't get in here.

The wind began howling outside, and even in the dining room, they could hear and feel debris beginning to pepper the house.

116

CHAPTER FIFTEEN

*I*t was late. The ghosts had raged on and off all day, and Johnny hoped to God they'd be quiet for a little while tonight. He was the only one up, on kind of an unofficial first watch. It was only nine-thirty, but it was smart to catch a couple of hours while it was quiet.

He was skimming volumes in the library, hoping to stumble upon an ancient ghost removal guide when Maya came in. She had two steaming cups, one of her herbal brews, no doubt.

"This will help you sleep."

"I don't want to sleep. I want to get rid of this damn ghost and find my grandfather."

Maya met Johnny's eyes and hers were round. "He's taken off before, though."

"Overnight. Sometimes a weekend, but not like this. Not since I've known him, anyway." Then he said, "But you've known him longer."

"Yeah. And he's taken off before, but he always left word where he'd be."

"Did he stop answering calls?"

"I don't know that anyone was calling him," she said. Then she said, "Should we start…checking hospitals, do you think?"

"I don't want to think it. Not yet."

"What about tracking his phone?"

"His ancient, no-internet flip phone?"

"Crap, I forgot."

"The lieutenant has the number, so if it can be done, she'll probably do it."

"We can get his photo out there, too, if she doesn't learn anything. I can do that online, get my followers to share it and spread the word. If you want."

He nodded, considering it. "I think he might hate that."

"I know he would. He's not used to having family around, no one to answer to. So maybe we save social media as a last resort?" She watched his face for a moment, and said, "Try not to think the worst, Johnny."

"I'm not."

"Yes, you are. It's in your eyes." She was looking into said eyes as she said it, and the gaze-to-gaze contact was electric and as visceral as a touch.

She blinked and didn't lock on again. Instead, she went to the sitting area with her tea and sat down. He followed and sat down as well. She took a sip of her tea, and he took a sip of his. He looked at the cup and then at her.

"Why are you feeling so guilty? she asked.

"I don't feel guilty. Why would I feel guilty? *He's* the one who left almost as soon as I got here."

"Mm-hm," she said and sipped more tea.

"I'm really angry with him," Johnny said. "And now it looks like something might've happened to him." He leaned back as if someone had pushed his chest. "You're right. I feel guilty."

"There it is."

He smiled at her. "Are you that intuitive, or do you just know me that well?"

"We've only known each other a few months, so I guess I'm that intuitive. Look, you have every right to be angry with him for taking off on you like that. And if something has happened to him, you couldn't have known."

He took that in and nodded.

"Guilt is a wasted emotion. You can let it go and move on. And I have new grist for your mill, Johnny. Maybe he had reasons for leaving, reasons we don't know about. And maybe he has reasons for being off the radar. We are assuming the worst, but there are dozens, maybe hundreds of variables. We can't assume anything."

"I guess you're right."

"I'll take the second watch, okay? Drink your tea and get a little sleep. You'll think better with a clear mind."

Johnny took a drink of the tea, and realized it was really good so he took another. Then he said, "I'll never sleep."

"Yes, you will." She nodded at his mug, and then at her own. "And I won't."

The next storm came at 4 a.m. and Kiley was about ready to tear out her hair. She sat up in bed, swearing. She'd slept in sweatpants, t-shirt, and socks for quick action. One simply *needed* socks for quick action. Slam your feet into shoes and you're ready to run. Try battling ghosts without socks sometime, and you'll understand.

Jack got up too, pulling his clothes on more slowly as Kiley went to the window to look outside, but it was too dark to see much. The wind was howling. There was thunder and lightning, but no rain.

Jack pulled her into his arms for what she thought was a sexy embrace. It turned out to be something else. "You're not safe so close to the window," he said, moving her aside.

"*You're* not safe," she replied as the storm howled louder. Then, when he obligingly hugged her like he ought to, "We have to fix this before somebody ends up dead. Somebody else, I mean."

"Agreed. Come on." He took her hand, and his was large and warm, and somehow she felt everything would be okay as long as she could touch him.

They emerged from their room to find everyone else doing the same, and headed for the library on autopilot. It was where they worked.

Chris was the first one in, and he flipped the light switch. Nothing happened. He looked behind him, and said, "Power's out."

"There are oil lamps on the book case," Maya said.

"Wait, those things work?" Kiley asked. "I thought you just brought them over for accent pieces."

"I thought they'd be nice at Yuletide. The one with the green oil is pine-scented, and the red is bayberry. And then everything happened and I never got around to lighting them." She walked past Chris and into the darkness. It startled Kiley for a second, how it had seemed to swallow her up, and she looked Johnny's way, because the Johnny Maya—Jaya?—saga was as riveting as it was frustrating.

Amen, sister!

Kiley stood motionless. She was vaguely aware of the yellow glow of one oil lamp, then the other, then of everyone moving past her into what she still thought of as a library, and Chris called their lair.

She looked around, but didn't see her house ghost. "Look, house ghost, if I'm the only one who can hear you, we might as well get to know each other, right?"

There was no reply. Then something slammed into the side of the house, the impact like a rifle crack that echoed in her chest and she added, "Later," and rushed into the library with the others.

The room was entirely transformed. Jack and Rodney from across the street had put plywood over the French doors and large windows to prevent more of them from being broken. It had the added benefit of making it bearable to work in there again, even if it did have a tomblike feel now.

Chris went to the computer bar in the back and fired up a laptop. "I have a full battery charge and internet."

"I've found a couple of books we didn't check," Maya said.

Kiley said, "No, guys, look, all this research is getting us nowhere. We have to *do* something."

"Well, I do have one idea," Chris said, closing the laptop and spinning on the tall stool.

Maya met his eyes and shook her head. "That's a bad idea, Chris."

It was amazing how she did that sometimes, Kiley thought, and then she looked to see if Johnny had been suitably impressed. Yep, poor guy looked spellbound.

"What's a bad idea?" Kiley asked at length. "Spill."

Shrugging a shoulder, Chris said a single word. "Seance."

"Wait, wait, what now?" Johnny held up a stop sign hand. "We're trying to keep them out and you want us to call them in?"

"*Seance*," Jack said, drawing the word out long and nodding his head.

"Not them," Chris said. "Benji." And he looked toward Breia and Ryan, who'd stayed silent until now.

They stood near each other in the corner closest to the doorway out into the hall. They looked terrified.

"The baby brother I never knew I had?" Breia said.

"Maybe we can get him to help us convince Robert and Mindi to cross over," Chris said. "If they're in-between the worlds, we're on one side and he's on the other. Maybe we can tag-team it and pry them loose."

"Or lovingly make them see reason," Maya said.

"Or figure out how to kick their spectral asses through the pearly gates." Kiley got up, too. "I think we should go for it. I mean, we're at a stand-still otherwise."

"I'm in," Maya said.

"Me, too," Jack said. "Johnny?"

Johnny looked at the others. "I don't like it, but I trust you guys. Okay. Let's do this."

Jack grabbed a lamp and led a parade back through the living room and into the dining room. "It might be dangerous for you two to be in the room for this," he told Breia and Ryan. "You should head upstairs to your rooms until it's over."

They looked at each other, then back at him. Breia crossed her arms over her chest. "You're kidding, right? You're going to try to talk the baby brother I didn't know I had, and you think I'm not staying in the room for it?"

Ryan crossed his arms in exactly the same way. "What she said."

Kiley fell a little bit in love with the stubborn shits.

CHAPTER SIXTEEN

*J*ohnny picked a chair and sat down to prepare himself. He tried to quiet his mind and open his senses. His grandfather had meditated every morning in the few weeks Johnny had lived with him, called it his "daily attunement." He'd cajoled the old man into teaching him how.

Kiley opened a drawer in the antique buffet and pulled out a white tablecloth. While she spread it, Maya opened a different drawer to remove white candles, holders, and a lighter. Then Jack set the sewn-up teddy bear and the baby picture onto the table too.

"I agree that Breia and Ryan should stay," Maya said. They're the same blood. It will help us connect." She looked around and everyone nodded in agreement.

"Then take a seat," she said to them. "There and there." She nodded toward the head and foot of the table, leaving only one empty seat for her. She moved the extra chair that didn't match into the spot between Chris and Johnny and sat down. He was glad. If there was a fight, he wanted her beside him.

Jack and Kiley sat across from them on the other side.

Maya lit the candles, closed her eyes. "Take a deep breath in, as one," she said. Her voice had gone softer and deeper. Johnny opened his eyes to watch her. Sometimes, when she was doing magical things, he could almost detect a golden glow around her, one that was only visible if he didn't look at it directly.

"And exhale," she said. After they'd done that a few times, she clasped Johnny's hand. "Hand to hand, we cast the circle."

"Hand to hand," Johnny said. He was looking right at her. "And heart to heart."

Her eyes opened and met his. They got all tangled up together for a minute, and he forgot to breathe for a millisecond before he turned to his left, where he took Breia's hand. "Hand to hand we cast the circle." And then he whispered, "Pass it on."

"Hand to hand we cast the circle," she said, reaching for Jack's hand. And the magic moved from Jack to Kiley to Ryan to Chris to Maya where it had begun as hands were clasped and words spoken.

Maya took a deep breath, opened her eyes. "We are between the worlds. Go ahead, Jack."

Jack kept his eyes closed, but everyone else had opened theirs. He'd been doing this sort of thing from the back room of The Magic Shop for years, but for most of that time, he'd believed himself a fraud, doling out psychologically sound advice disguised as advice from the dead. He knew his shit.

"I'm speaking to the spirit Benji Sousa, brother of Breia and Ryan. Child of Mindi and Robert. Come to us. You are welcome here."

Johnny felt suddenly cold, like a door had opened on winter. He looked around the room, but it was dim. The shadows danced with every candle flicker.

"Benji, we need your help. Please hear us and answer."

"Oh, shit, you've done it now!" Kiley rose up to her feet as those words exploded from her in a voice that was not hers. It was deeper and had a raspy quality. "You've opened the door!"

Her hair was blowing back but there was no wind in the room. The candle flames burned tall and straight. Johnny could see how hard Jack was clasping her hand. "Ryan," he said, "Don't let go of Kiley's hand."

"Don't break the circle," Maya cried.

Kiley fell into her chair as if all her bones had left her body. Her head fell forward, and suddenly Maya rose to her feet and opened her eyes, and they were black.

Breia screamed, backing away from the table, pulling her hands free, breaking the circle.

"My children. At last."

"M-m-mother?" Breia could see what Johnny could, the image superimposed over Maya's face, the image of a different woman, with dark hair, hollow eyes, a face of melting wax.

Maya-not-Maya looked at Breia and smiled. "So strong. Always, so strong." And then she looked up, "Husband, what takes you so long?"

And all of the sudden Johnny passed out. Or that's what it felt like.

Kiley said, "What the fuck is happening here? Johnny? What are you doing?" She watched Johnny rise from his chair and turn to gaze at Maya. And then he wrapped her in his arms and kissed her like the end of a romance novel.

"Holy shit," Jack said. Then he looked at Kiley, then at them again, then at Kiley. Then he said, "Oh. *Now* I get it."

She rolled her eyes.

When they split apart, the face kind of masking Johnny's smiled at Ryan. "We cannot protect you if you stay here, do you understand, son?"

"Yeah. That's why I'm here. And I'm not leaving this house."

"Not here in this house. Here in this *form*."

"Be with us," said whoever was speaking with Maya's mouth. "Leave this life behind. You belong with us."

Ryan backed around the table, behind Jack and Kiley, all the way to his sister. She got up and put her arms around him. "Be with you, as in, *dead* like you?" His voice cracked when he said it.

"We're not dead," said the ghost of the boy's mother. And she laughed softly, looking at Johnny, who laughed too. "We're right here. You can see we're not dead."

"But you will be," Chris said, rising and waving his arms to draw their attention. "Listen up. A soul has to either occupy a physical body or cross over and reunite with its Source. If you stay disconnected, you'll break your own cycle. You'll disintegrate and rejoin the Universe as energy."

"Ryan is doing well," Breia cried. "He has a future, a life ahead of him. He'll have a wife someday, and children. You would really deny him all that?"

"We must protect him!" They shouted, the voice a distorted bellow coming from a warped LP

"Because you didn't protect Benji?" Jack asked.

Maya threw back her head and wailed, and every single person in the room cowered. Ryan and Breia backed all the way into a corner, hugging each other and trembling.

"That's just about e-fucking-nuff!" Kiley shouted. "Bitch, get outta my friend." But Maya's wails changed to sobs, and she started toward Breia and Ryan. Kiley grabbed the fireplace poker and jumped in front of them, jabbing it with manace and cussing like a sailor.

"Tell me about Benji" Jack said, in full-on shrink voice. All calm and sympathetic. "Tell me about your first son."

The ghost in Johnny howled in grief, grabbed Jack's hand and closed his black eyes, and then Johnny blinked out and Jack dropped like a sack of feed and lay twitching on the floor.

"Jack!" Kiley shrieked. She couldn't run to him, because she had to keep Maya off the kids. She had no idea what the crazy bitch possessing her would do if she got to them. "Chris!"

"I've got them!" Chris lunged over there and knelt beside Jack, clasped his shoulders and rolled him onto his back but he couldn't seem to wake him up. "Why hasn't Johnny blinked back yet?" he asked.

～

Johnny blipped into a hospital, in a large room full of miniature babies in incubation units.

"So tiny, so helpless," a man said. Johnny turned to see Robert Sousa standing beside his wife. They were dressed in scrubs, with paper covers over their shoes. They wore face masks, and their gloved hands were clasped. The man's other hand was pressed against the surface of a warm plexiglass bed with a baby inside. It was sideways, his hand, its heel near the baby's feet, its fingertips well beyond the baby's head.

He took it all in as he ducked behind a curtain. He saw a stack of masks, grabbed one and quickly put it on. He didn't know how this stuff worked, but he didn't want to make a bunch of premies sick with germs from the future.

"You have been here non-stop for three weeks," a nurse said. "We've bent the rules so far, but enough is enough, Mr. and Mrs. Sousa. You have to go home. Get a decent meal and some rest. Come back tomorrow.

"No, we can't leave him," Mindi cried.

"It wasn't a request. You're doing him no good here. We've made exceptions for you so far, because of your extreme..." She cleared her throat. "Devotion. But normal visiting hours are back in force, and they have ended. You have a little girl. Go home to her. Come back in the morning."

"But–"

"Go home." She walked away.

Robert slid his hand over his wife's elbow and said, "Let's go." And when she shot him a look, he leaned down as if to kiss her cheek and whispered as Johnny strained to hear. "The shifts change in two hours. We'll come right back."

Johnny blinked back into the present. Chris was kneeling over Jack, who was prone on the floor. Across the room Kiley was menacing Maya with a fireplace poker while Breia and Ryan cowered behind her. Chris helped Jack up onto his feet. And when Johnny met Jack's eyes, he knew Jack had witnessed that scene in the neonatal ICU.

Then he was sure, when Jack said, "A nurse made them leave the ICU where they'd been glued for three weeks. When they went back, Benji was dead."

Johnny listened while inching around the room toward Maya, who was still being held within the dark, filmy aura of Mindi Sousa's ghost.

A deep, inhuman voice filled the house to the rafters, then. "If you think we will leave another child behind, you have miscalculated the depths of our love."

"You're trying to kill your kids, Robert. That's not love," Jack said.

Johnny kept going. When he was close enough to Maya, and still unseen, he propelled himself forward and wrapped his arms around her. She struggled and roared, but he. Held on. "I've got you, Maya. I know you're in there, come on now, come on and show this bitch who's boss."

Maya scrunched up her face, and then shouted, "Get out get out get out get out GET *OUUUUUT*!" Then she went limp in his arms, sighed heavily and leaned into him.

Kiley stepped closer and jabbed Maya's shoulder with the poker. Maya lifted her head to glare at her. Johnny's arms were still around her, but he let go once she had her footing. She was herself again.

Maya narrowed her eyes on Kiley. "What were you going to do with that? Skewer me?"

"Maybe. A little." Kiley dropped the poker onto the hearthstone.

Maya turned to Johnny. "Thanks for bringing me back."

"Thanks for coming back."

Everyone looked around the room. There was a sensation of lightness again. The dense, dark energy of those two was gone.

CHAPTER SEVENTEEN

"We opened the door," Kiley said.

"Yeah, so the house ghost told us through your mouth." Chris made a face and nodded when she looked at him like he was crazy.

"What are you talking about?"

"She did," Chris told her. "You did. You said we'd opened the door but it didn't sound like you."

She frowned, looking around the room. Everyone nodded affirmation. "Was it a kind of raspy voice? Like this?" She tried to mimic the ghost she'd heard. And when they all nodded, she said, "That was her all right."

"Looks like you're going woo-woo," Chris said, all excited. "I'm going to be the only muggle left."

"Yeah, don't jump to conclusions," she said.

Jack moved closer and put his hands on her shoulders. "Are you still okay?"

"I'm still…digesting it, I guess."

"At least now we know why they're so obsessed with Ryan," Johnny said.

"Benji was premature," Breia said. "I remember that summer, but only vaguely. I stayed with friends of theirs who were strangers to me. I didn't know where my parents had gone or why and I was afraid they would never come back."

"I was premature, too, right?" Ryan said.

"Yes, yes, only by about six weeks," Breia said, sliding an arm around her brother. "They never left your side. Not even after they brought you home. I was ten, and I remember thinking they had forgotten all about me, they were so obsessed with you."

"I'm sorry, Breia," he said, and hugged her.

"Don't be. It wasn't your fault."

Jack was pacing and thinking aloud. "Your mother died so soon after all that. She died with all that guilt and grief still unprocessed in her. And then there was your father, left with all of that plus the loss of his wife, the only other person he'd been as obsessed with as he was with Ryan."

"Tell me you're not making excuses for them," Kiley said.

"I'm just trying to understand them better," Jack said. "They were already on this dark, downward spiral of guilt and loss and crippling grief when they died, and they couldn't let go of it to move on. You have to leave all that behind to move on, right?" Jack was on a roll. Kiley loved what a geek he was when he got hold of a new theory.

"One would assume, yeah," Johnny said. "So they couldn't let it go. They couldn't move on. And then they latched onto baby Ryan."

"He might've even felt like an anchor for a while," Maya said. "They might've even come to need him in order to stay earthbound."

"Yeah, they need me so much they'll happily kill me to keep me with them," Ryan said. "Which kind of negates their whole motivation, where they think if they leave my side, I'll die." He rolled his eyes.

Chris walked a few steps away, hands moving near his head.

"Okay, good. We know where we are. The parental ghosts have gone homicidal and our fearless leader might be possessed by a house ghost. So, we won't run out of problems, in case anyone was worried about that."

"Not possessed. I can just hear her. Wait, I'm the leader?"

"Of course you're the leader," Chris said.

And Jack said, "I thought I was the leader."

Kiley looked around. "Looks like they wore themselves out."

"But they'll keep coming back." Ryan looked hopeless.

"We need more powerful magic than any of us have," Maya said. "I don't know what to do next."

Johnny's phone chirped. He pulled it from his pocket and his face lit up. "It's my grandfather!"

His grandfather's photo was on the top of the text message screen. He'd snapped one on his phone, because there was no online album for John Redhawk. His forebear did not do social media.

The message from his grandfather's phone asked, "Are you a friend or relative of whoever owns this phone?"

Johnny's blood seemed to rush to his feet. He tapped back his reply, a simple yes, and the phone rang right after.

"It's someone else using his phone," he told the others, and then he answered and put the phone on speaker so they could hear. They were probably closer to his grandfather than he was.

"I'm calling from the One-Stop on Old River Road. This phone was left in our restroom. I saw you'd called so I figured you might know who owns it."

"It's my grandfather John Redhawk's phone. I'm trying to locate him. Did you see him? He's native, seventy I think, usually wears his hair tied back. It's mostly gray."

"I'm sorry, I don't remember seeing anyone like that. He's missing you say?"

"Do you know how long the phone has been there?"

"Could be a week." He didn't add that was how often the restrooms were cleaned, but Johnny had a feeling.

"Listen, I can't come and get it right now–" Maya and Breia both objected and he held up a traffic cop hand. "Keep it safe for me I'll give you a reward when I pick it up."

"How much?"

"Fifty bucks."

"Hundred."

He'd have to use money from the account he'd sworn not to touch, the one his mom and step-father funded. But he could swallow his pride for his grandfather. "Done."

"Okay. Come when you can."

"It'll only be a day or two. I hope."

"He's missing, huh?" The guy said. Then, "There's a voicemail message on the home screen. Might be something that could help find your grandad."

"It might. Can you play it for me?"

Everyone in the room leaned in closer, and there was a collective gasp when they heard John Redhawk's voice.

"Grandson, there are things I must do alone, just now. But I am with you, even while I am away. My visions have shown me the dark spirits you face. Get my journals. You were with me when we hid them. Something in them will help you." His voice went suddenly lower. "I will return to Burnt Hills and to you. I love you, Johnny, and I'm proud to be your grandfather." The phone beeped to signal the end of the message.

Johnny looked around the room, then at the phone in his hand. "Shit, I should've recorded it. Can you play it again?"

"I got it, Johnny." Maya held up her phone.

"All right. Okay. Thank you, Mr. uh—"

"Barney," he said.

"Mr. Barney. That helps more than you know."

They disconnected and Johnny just stood there for a minute trying to process his grandfather's words.

"He's okay," Maya said. "He's okay. And he had reasons for taking off that had nothing to do with any of us. Personal reasons."

Jack shook his head as if astounded. "He's still helping us, even though he's not here. He's somehow getting visions of what's going on with us."

"Quantum entanglement," Chris said. "Once two particles have interacted, they maintain a connection even far apart. You poke one, the other flinches."

"Are you shitting me?" Kiley looked at him in disbelief.

"Einstein called it 'spooky action at a distance.' Aptly named, I think."

Kiley smiled at him and said, "I am so glad the nerdiest nerd in all Nerdville is *our* nerd."

Johnny's head was spinning. He couldn't seem to latch onto any one thing.

Everyone had drifted away from the tight grouping, except for Maya. She leaned nearer him and said very softly, "He's okay. And he loves you and is proud of you. I don't think you have to worry about him."

He nodded, but something niggled in his brain. "Will you send that recording to my phone?"

"If you'll text Mendosa and tell her to call off the missing persons thing."

Johnny tapped a text to the lieutenant and hit send. "Done."

Maya tipped her screen up, tapped it and said, "Done."

Johnny's phone pinged to prove it. "Thanks." Then he looked around at the others. "I have to go get the journals. We're out of ideas, and he says they'll have what we need."

Kiley nodded. "You're right, you have to."

"Yes, and now, right this minute," Maya said. "If we leave while the ghosts are recuperating–"

"What do you mean, we?" Johnny asked.

"I mean I'm going with you, is what I mean. Duh. I'm very fond of John, and I'm worried about him, and frankly, I've known him longer than you have." She averted her eyes. "Besides, nobody should be going anywhere alone until we've sent the Sousas to the other side."

"I hate this," Chris said. "Splitting up the gang like this."

"It's not that far," Johnny said.

"Actually, you'll go right by the gas station where John's phone was found on the way," Jack said. "Might as well pick it up while you're out."

"All right." Johnny went to Breia and Ryan, who stood side by side. He put one hand on Breia's shoulder, the other on Ryan's. "I am not abandoning you, I swear. I am coming right back, and I hope I'll be bringing the solution to all this. So you can have your lives back."

"I'll be having mine for the first time," Ryan said.

"Go," Breia told him. "We're safe here."

He looked at Ryan. His face was shuttered. "You guys are family, now," Johnny said.

"It's true," Maya agreed. "I mean, we get close with our clients—"

"I had lunch with a snotty-ass Patell twin just last week," Kiley put in.

"We get close with our clients," Maya repeated. "But with you guys, it's more."

"It's personal, poking around a person's ghosts." Jack nodded as he spoke. "I can't think of anything more personal, really. Generations deep sort of personal. And this one just feels like that times ten."

"And we feel what you're going through," Johnny said.

"There's a connection that's made. I can't explain it better than that."

"Quantum entanglement," Chris said.

～

Kiley saw Maya signal her with her eyes while Johnny was still talking. Then she headed for the kitchen, so Kiley quietly followed.

Maya was taking two travel mugs from the cupboard, but she turned around to face Kiley when she came in. "So, if we're doing this girlfriend thing—"

"Which we are," Kiley said.

Maya inhaled, nodded, and filled the mugs from the always-fresh pot. "I think Johnny's holding back from moving forward with Breia because he thinks he wants me."

"Thinks he wants you?" Kiley asked. "Don't you think he *knows* what he wants?"

"Don't you think he'd be better off with Breia than me?" Maya countered.

"Why, for God's sake?" Kiley lifted her palms, shoulders and eyebrows as one.

"Oh, I don't know. She's young. She can reproduce. He wouldn't be facing widower status in his fifties."

"So you're already married and considering a family in this scenario," Kiley said, and it wasn't a question.

Maya added cream and sugar to one mug, stirred and then screwed on both lids. "I'm just trying to consider all the repercussions. I'll die and leave him alone."

"That's dumb. You're a vegan, you'll live into triple digits."

Maya set the mugs down and paced away, pushing her blond hair back over her head. "And what about having children someday?"

"Women have kids in their forties, Maya."

"Yeah, not this one. My fallopian tubes have been tied and burned and sealed by magic." She lowered her head. "My gyno said childbirth could kill me. So…"

"Oh." Kiley shrugged. "Well, look, people adopt. Or get surrogates. Don't even look my way on that one, though." She glanced at her reflection in the stainless steel toaster. "I mean, I know my womb is a ten, but I don't rent it out."

Lady El popped into the toaster right beside her and made her jump. She wore the same dress, but this time there were sparkly colored glass butterflies clipped through her hair and her cigarette holder was white.

If she lets that hot young stallion go, I will haunt her to the ends of the earth. Tell her.

"Lady El thinks you shouldn't let Johnny get away."

That is not what I said.

Kiley rolled her eyes, and lowered her head. "Fine, I'll translate verbatim. 'Maya, if you let that hot young stallion get away I will haunt you.'"

Maya laughed. It was kind of a sad laugh, though. "I like our house ghost."

"She likes you too, which is why she's giving you such good advice."

"Good for me, maybe. Bad for Johnny." Maya sighed. "But he's not going to accept that unless I do something drastic."

"Like what?" Kiley asked.

Maya crooked a finger at her, and Kiley moved closer. Maya leaned in and whispered her idea into Kiley's ear. Kiley just closed her eyes and shook her head and thought it the worst notion ever.

~

Johnny clapped Ryan's shoulder. "Just…stay safe until we get back. And maybe come up with an idea, in case this doesn't pan out, huh?" He looked at the others as he said that, then gave a nod at Maya, but she and Kiley were no longer where they'd been a minute ago.

They re-appeared though, Maya holding two travel mugs. "I figured while you were speechifying, I had time to grab some java. You ready now?" She exchanged a look with Kiley, who sent one back that he couldn't read.

He opened the door for Maya and she went out before him and headed for the truck. It was still dark outside. Dawn was hours away, and there was debris everywhere. No damage to the house this time. Everything loose enough to be flung at it had been flung at it.

He saw the flashing lights of repair trucks, and men working on the power lines on the corner.

Maya went to the passenger side of the truck where he waited to open the door, since her hands were full with both mugs.

He reached past her to do so and then relieved her of one of the coffees. "Thanks. I need this."

"Me, too." She popped her mug into the cup holder, buckled her seatbelt and shut her door as he went around the truck's nose and got behind the wheel. He took a sip before he set the cup down, then said, "Perfect."

"I have a good memory."

"I do, too." He let his eyes hold hers for a second, hoping she'd see the memory he referred to smoldering there. That night on her sofa, when they'd been watching a movie and had almost kissed. He'd leaned in, and she'd tilted her head and parted her lips just a little. He was so close his lips brushed hers, and then she pulled back, and pretended it hadn't happened.

He'd have married her that night.

The still small voice of reason whispered in his ear, *Don't you think that was the point of her brake-pumping?*

Oh. He almost said it out loud, blinked, and decided to

consider it later, as he drove toward his grandfather's apartment without a ghost in sight.

Maya sat on the passenger seat, looking out the window at the darkness of late March. Her face was a portrait of ease. He understood it, and he felt exactly the same way. Relieved. Safe, even if only temporarily. They were clear of the ghosts.

"It's more than the attacks, I think," he said.

She nodded, knowing what he meant. "It's their anger. It hits us as hard as their freak storms and earthquakes do. Harder, maybe."

"Hate's invisible but I think it's potentially lethal."

"Preach." She held up a hand-to-God, smiling at him, trying to lighten him up. "How are you doing?" she asked when it didn't work.

"It hurts that he left. I just found him. The only blood relative I have on my birth-father's side, as far as I know. And he just leaves and lies about where he's going." He tried to rein in his emotions. It wasn't like him to let them run free like that.

"But now we know his leaving had nothing to do with you. And it sounds like it was something important."

"Like what, though?"

"I don't know. He had a whole long life that we know nothing about, right?"

He looked at her, then back at the road. And then he said, "I never thought of it that way. You're right."

"Well, that's why it's good to have a friend to kick things around with."

She settled back in her seat, watching the road, content and quiet.

"Is that what we are now?" he asked softly. "Friends?"

It took long seconds for her to say, "I'd like us to try to be. Can we, do you think?"

"I don't know." His feelings for her hadn't changed. Even though they'd only hung out for a few weeks, it had left him wanting more, and then she'd just seemed to back off. It was over almost before it had begun. And she was trying to act like it was no big deal, because *they* had been no big deal.

But this didn't feel like something minor or small to him. It felt like something inevitable. She pulled at him like nobody ever had. Like magic.

"I'll try," he said. But what he meant was, *I'll keep on aching for you and pretending not to.*

CHAPTER EIGHTEEN

$\mathcal{H}$is grandfather's place was on the second floor of a red brick, turn-of-the-century building. The first floor housed the local dive, Quincy's Bar, which was closed this early in the morning. It was still gray and pre-dawn.

He had his grandfather's phone in his pocket. They'd stopped at the gas station where it had been found in hopes Mr. Barney would still be on shift and he was. Johnny had shown the old man a photo of his grandfather, hoping it would spark a memory. Instead, it seemed to spark his generosity. He'd had a change of heart, he said, and refused his reward.

Johnny parked the truck along the roadside in front and they got out. The sun hadn't come up yet, and the sidewalk was damp with dew. He noticed Maya looking around, probably on the lookout for ghosts. So far there was no sign of trouble, though.

"There's a side stair," he said, leading her into the alley, where an enclosed stairway clung like an ugly scab to the side of the building. He went up, and Maya followed. The stairway was dark as pitch. At the top he found the spare key in the knothole where his grandfather kept it, unlocked the door, walked inside and flipped on the lights.

It wasn't a large space. Living room and kitchen open, bedroom and bathroom walled off. There was a yellow formica table with looped stainless legs, a TV that still had a picture tube and was hooked to a VCR. The ancient plaid sofa sagged deep but didn't sport a rip, tear, or stain.

Maya looked around in dismay at all the shelves and stands, packed and stacked with boxes, books and papers.

"You think that's bad, just wait til I open the closets," Johnny said.

"Johnny, time is of the essence here."

"I know."

"It'll take us all day to search this place. Let's listen to the message again, maybe there's a clue."

Maya tapped her phone and replayed the message. It got all the way to "Find my journals. You were with me when we hid them," before she paused the playback. "There, right there. You were with him when he hid them."

"Only I wasn't. I've never seen him hide anything, and I didn't even know he kept journals. I don't know why he'd say that."

"It's weird too that he didn't just say where they were. Or why they needed hiding to begin with," she said.

She frowned in confusion and played the rest of the message, frowning. Johnny headed into the bedroom to start searching there. He sat on the edge of bed and looked around the room, as if that would give him a clue where to begin.

Immediately, he felt that falling sensation. Only when he landed he was exactly where he'd been before. Just when he thought he hadn't blipped at all, his grandfather stepped into the room. He was carrying a box in his arms, but he stopped when he saw Johnny, who'd jumped to his feet, startled.

His grandfather wasn't old. His hair was dark, with almost no gray at all, and his face was chiseled and handsome. He looked at Johnny, frowning. "What are you doing in my bed?" Then he frowned harder. "You look like me."

"I'm your grandson," Johnny said. His father hadn't died until he was three years old, so Johnny had known his grandfather for that small amount of time, before his mom had remarried and moved him away. He didn't remember any of it, but he'd pieced it together while trying to locate blood relatives from his dad's side.

John's dark brows rose. He squinted and looked closer. "Johnny?" he asked. "All grown up?" Then he nodded slowly. "This is some kind of magic."

"Yes. You told me to find your journals. That's why I'm here."

John looked down at the box he carried. "These journals?"

"I don't know. Maybe. You said I was with you when you hid them."

"And so you are here, right now. I am hiding them for *you*."

"That's a heckofa coincidence."

"There are no such things, grandson. From the looks of you, there will be many more journals in this box by the time you come back to find them."

"I need to know where you're hiding them," Johnny said.

His grandfather shrugged. "Then hide them yourself." He shoved the box into Johnny's hands.

Johnny looked around the room for a hiding place.

"Wait," his grandfather said. "Add this to the box. It's important, too." He pulled an old record album from the closet shelf and set it on top of the box.

"Why?" Johnny asked.

"I don't know."

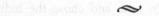

Kiley should be cheerful. The sun was up, and it was a bright and beautiful, early spring day. The birds were singing, the grass was greening up, and there wasn't a single patch of filthy leftover snow left in sight.

None of them had gone back to bed after the last attack.

Johnny and Maya had left to search John's apartment for his journals. Ryan was on the front porch, gaming on his phone, maybe needing to be outside while there was a chance. Breia was up in her room. Chris was manning the computers in search of arcane knowledge.

Kiley sat beside Jack on the little sofa in the office, skimming books, with the French doors open wide to let the spring warmth in.

It was not a quiet morning, despite the ghosts' absence. There were road crews out front using jackhammers to break up the demolished pavement. Others were manning chainsaws to clean up toppled trees, and the power company guys had sent two truckloads of workers to replace a snapped-in-half power pole and re-string the wires and cables it had held. They'd closed down the whole block.

"Local news says it was a microburst," Jack said, reading from his phone. "What they can't get over is that it's the second, or according to some of the neighbors, third in the very same location."

The phone he was looking at rang. "It's Maya." He tapped to answer and said, "Hi, Maya. You're on speaker."

"So are you. How are things?" she asked. "Ghosts been acting out?"

"Not yet, and it's longer than usual," Kiley said. "I wonder if all the repair crews are putting them off."

"Have you found the journals?" Jack asked.

"Yes, a whole box full." That was Johnny's voice.

"Johnny blipped back in time and chose the hiding place above a ceiling panel, which is why John said he as there when they were hidden," Maya said. "And yes, thinking about that too much *will* give you a headache."

"Is there anything in them that will help?"

"We'll go through them when we get back," Johnny said. "We figured we should get them to headquarters as soon as possible, before another outburst. Listen, though, just before I came back to the present, Grandfather put an old LP record on top of the box and said it was important."

Maya said, "The album cover has a gorgeous redhead draped across a piano. Lady El, *'Round Midnight.*"

Loud as a siren, right in Kiley's ear, the house ghost let loose a whoop and said, *The hell you say! That old fart is a fan? Who'd have known he had taste like that?*

Kiley looked around, her eyes wide, her face frozen. "Okay," she said, "in case no one else heard all that–"

"Heard what?" Jack asked.

"I think Lady El is our house ghost."

"Sending photo," Maya said, and a few seconds later, the album cover came through Kiley's phone.

"Yes, that's her, minus twenty years and twenty-five pounds."

Watch yourself, toots.

From the computer, Chris said, "Should I start a database of our otherworldly contacts?"

"I think maybe it's time you try to communicate with the house ghost, Kiley," Maya said.

"But I'm not–"

"You're the one she's connecting to. And apparently, she can help."

Jack and Chris nodded in agreement.

After the phone call, Kiley turned to Jack. "I don't know how to begin. I don't want to try another seance, that's for sure."

"What about…?" Jack went to the bookshelf and reached up to the top to pull down a really nice wooden spirit board. Its letters were hand-painted, its edges, raised and beveled to keep the planchette from overshooting the sides the way it tended to do at teenage slumber parties. The wood was thick, and every inch of the sides were engraved with the faces of demons and angels and fairies and all sorts of whimsical creatures.

Its planchette was also wooden, apparently hand-carved, and engraved with the sun and the moon. It held a small glass circle in its center.

Kiley thought it was both beautiful and scary. "I didn't know we had that."

"I brought it from the shop," Jack said. "It was a display piece. Not for sale. Very old, though it comes with more stories than provenance." He set it on the little coffee table, and in a conspiratorial whisper said, "It's said to have been used by Madame Blavatsky."

"You say that like I know who she is." Kiley leaned over the board and touched the wooden surface. It was smooth, its letters painted in white and edged in gold on a dark wood surface.

"It's beautiful," she said. "But um... I'm a little bit afraid of it."

"That's okay," Chris called. "My spirit board is better." He looked their way from the computer bar. "That would be my keyboard, in case you didn't get it."

"We got it," Jack said, even though Kiley didn't think they had. "What did you find, Chris?"

"I'll read it aloud. 'Lady El, born Eleonore Petrenko, was a jazz singer throughout the late forties and early fifties. She performed in clubs all up and down the east coast from New York City to the Outer Banks, but her heart belonged to Saratoga Springs and the surrounding communities.'" He looked at them over his computer glasses. "That would be us." Then he read on. "'Eventually she purchased a Victorian house in one such community where she retired and spent her waning years, all but housebound, with the exception of a brief and highly successful comeback tour in 1964. Some said she was at her best that year. When it ended, she returned to her beloved home. It's said she never left it again. Eleonore Petrenko died in her sleep in 1969. It is said her dying words to the nurse who cared for her at the end, were, "I told you I'd never leave this place.'"

"And she never did," Kiley said.

"Wait a minute, wait a minute," Chris said. *Tappity tap tap*. One final tap with a flourish and an ad for toothpaste came wafting from the speakers.

"Shoot. Just a sec. Skip ads, and…"

There was a sweet bluesy trumpet riff, and then the sultry opening lines of Thelonius Monk's "'Round Midnight" came in a deep, smoky voice that wept with emotion.

Kiley came to a slow stand and listened, mesmerized.

"That's her," she whispered.

"That's her," Chris said. He got up, too, and so did Jack. They listened, looking around the place as if they might spot her, but no one did. Eventually Breia came from upstairs, and Ryan from outside.

"Who is it?" Ryan whispered.

"House ghost," Chris replied, like it was an ordinary answer.

When the song ended, Kiley started to clap and nodded at the others, who did the same. Then they clapped louder, whistled and hooted. And when their applause finally petered out, Lady El said, *Well, you do know how to flatter a girl, I'll give you that much.*

Kiley turned slowly, as if toward her voice, except not really. And then she caught her reflected in the surface of her coffee. "It was wonderful," Kiley said. And the gang looked at her, then at each other, then they all tried to get a look inside her cup. "Eleonore–"

Lady El.

"Lady El, yes, of course. Do you know anything that can help us get those dark ghosts to move on?"

I've seen it before. You dally too long in this world without your body, you lose the part that knows the way over. There's no more knowing, then.

"She says if you don't cross when you die, you lose the part of you that knows the way." Then she frowned into her mug. "But you're without your body and not on the other side."

This place is my body. My soul's bound to this old house. It was my best friend for a long time. When the house is no more, I'll still know my way. I'm anchored, see? Not free-floating in a world where I don't belong, like those two are. I'm this house's soul now, until it dies. She started to sing a jazzed-up version of *Shall We Gather at the River.*

Kiley listened politely until she finished.

Jack said, "What did she say?"

"The house is her body until it's gone. Then she'll move on," Kiley said. "So, Lady El, how can we find someone to show these ghosts the way?"

In the mug, Lady El's reflection puffed her cigarette and blew the smoke. It rose from the mug like steam. But the coffee had cooled to lukewarm,

You can't. Some sucker they love has to die, find 'em, and lead 'em across. Has to be somebody fresh, you know? All lit up. And it has to be somebody who can light them up, too, cause it ain't gonna work unless it comes from within.

She stopped talking, and Kiley waited a beat, but she did not say more. "That's it? That's all you've got? Somebody they love has to die?"

Silence, so apparently that was a yes.

"How do you know about all this?"

It begins to tell 'round midnight, 'round midnight...

Her reflection vanished among the ripples and her voice slowly faded to silence.

Chris sneezed.

CHAPTER NINETEEN

*L*ater that afternoon, just before a planned nap, since they'd all been up most of the night, Kiley took the spirit board into the upstairs bathroom.

She wanted more, and she wanted it in private. This was *her* thing.

Shit had gone down in this bathroom, so she was a little creeped out. But it was still the best place to guarantee privacy. The lack of that commodity was one of the setbacks of her place becoming Spook Central headquarters. An expected one, though, and she still didn't regret it. There wouldn't usually be this degree of activity. She just needed to get through this case, and then tweak things a little bit. Carve out some time when her house was just her house.

She didn't know what the ever-loving hell she was doing as far as spirit boards were concerned, but she had to try.

The shower was running, cold water, because she didn't want to fill the room with steam or waste energy. The medicine cabinet light was on, but she'd draped a sheer scarf over it. That was as dark as she was willing to go in this room.

She sat on a folded towel on the floor, and put the spirit board in front of her, also on a folded towel. She figured it might be disrespectful to put it directly on the floor. Especially in a bathroom, no matter how clean.

She hadn't brought in any candles or incense. Those were more Maya's style. Kiley didn't even really want to use the board. It would be better if they could just talk.

She took a deep breath, closed her eyes, and said, "Whoever's out there who's good, all those I've helped, all love and light, be with me and keep me safe," which seemed pretty close to what Maya often said before mucking around in the spirit world. "No bad shit, though."

She opened one eye and things seemed perfectly normal, so she opened the other and placed her fingertips on the planchette. Three fingers from each hand felt natural, so she went with that. "Lady El, will you come and talk to me?"

The heavy planchette began to tremble beneath her fingers. Kiley widened her eyes and willed herself to keep her hands in place when everything in her wanted to jerk them away and run screaming from the room.

Somehow she stayed put and the thing stopped shaking and began to move. It made small circles, then wider ones, gliding over the board like skates over ice. And then it flew off the board and across the room, slamming into the back of the door.

And then somebody laughed really hard, and she got up to her feet and turned around at the same time.

There she was, Lady El, in the mirror, laughing so hard she had tears. *If you could've seen your face*, she said without moving her mouth. Each lock of her flame red hair was like a satin ribbon, artfully entwined with its fellows and piled high on top. Her lashes were as thick as if she'd glued paintbrushes to her eyelids. A half-inch boundary of eyeliner surrounded green eyes in a plump, pink-cheeked face. Her jawline showed signs of sag.

What? You've never seen true beauty before? she asked, and she took a drag from her cigarette in its long black holder. She wore gloves to her elbows, also black, and a red sequined dress with a neckline low enough to show her impressive cleavage.

"Lady El?"

Who the hell else?

Kiley smiled on the inside, inexplicably gratified that her house ghost was a sarcastic bitch. "I'm Kiley."

I know.

"Why am I the only one who can see you?"

She shrugged and took a puff. *You a medium?*

"No. My guy Jack is, but he can't see you. Maya's a witch and she can't see you. Johnny's got all sorts of woo-woo shit going on, but he can't see you. Why me? I'm just a muggle."

Woo-woo? Muggle?

"Supernatural abilities. Ordinary human."

Got it. The lingo's changed. Then she started to sing 'Round Midnight again.

"You're a wonderful singer," Kiley said.

Oh, you want to hear more? I take requests.

"Well, yes, but first I—"

The albums are in the attic, you know. Knock yourself out, toots. She looked down her nose, shrugged and said, *I suppose you can use the other things too, if you think they might help.*

"What other things?"

I'm more than just a singer, child. Way more. I mean, I am the soul of this house, and this house is... well, you know. She waved her fingers and puffed her cheroot, and sang a long, warbling goodbye while blowing the smoke right out of the mirror.

Kiley waved her hand and swore, then opened the bathroom window.

Tap tap on the door. Jack called, "You okay in there?"

"Fine, babe. Uh..." She turned off the shower knobs, picked up the spirit board and the wooden planchette and the little viewing glass circle that had popped out of its center. It hadn't broken, thank goodness. Then she opened the door and stepped into the bedroom where Jack was waiting.

He looked at her, then at the board, then at the bathroom. And then he sniffed the air. "You smoking in the girl's room or..."

"No."

He smiled like he was teasing her. "You know, if you want privacy, just tell me. You don't have to—"

"I know. I just felt dumb. You're the one with the powers and here I am trying to talk to this ghost. I just..."

She shrugged her shoulders and set the board on the bed.

"I'm sorry if it didn't work. It worked before. Maybe we could try together?"

"Oh, no, it worked," she said.

He drew back and lifted his eyebrows. "It did?"

"Not the board. I mean, she thought it was a joke, but she came through long enough to blow smoke in my face and tell me her albums are in the attic."

He lifted his brows like a kid who'd just been told there were limitless free cookies.

"Did you just hear her again, or...?"

"Saw her in the mirror. She's amazing. A sassy fifty-something with flame red hair. Long gloves, sequins, cigarette holder, the whole nine."

"That's amazing! This is incredible." He pulled back the covers. He already had one knee on the mattress. They'd discussed a power nap, since they'd been up most of the night. She looked at him like he had lobsters crawling out his ears. "Oh." He put the leg down. "We're going to the attic, aren't we?"

She just looked at him. He reached for his pants.

~

The attic. She'd been inside it precisely once, when the realtor had climbed up while showing her the house. To refuse to follow would have been to reveal herself as the bigger chicken shit. So naturally, Kiley had gone up.

There was a door in the upstairs hallway that could easily be mistaken as hiding a closet. But no, it hid the darkest and narrowest staircase in Saratoga County, possibly the entire state of New York. Even when you flicked the switch, the single bulb in the ceiling halfway up did little to light the way. Flashlights were not optional.

She and Jack each held one as they climbed the stairs, him first, her with one hand on his butt, for security. Mostly.

At the top there was another door that opened into a wide span of darkness with a light switch inside. Three bulbs came on spaced near, halfway and far. They gave a little more light to the gigantic area of mostly open space with sheet-draped shapes here and there.

"See the boards, crossing the floor?" Jack asked.

She nodded, noting the insulation-backing in between, stapled to said boards. "Walk only on those boards. If you step in between, you'll go right through the floor and punch a hole in the ceiling below. Okay?"

"Like you think I didn't see *Christmas Vacation*?" Kiley lifted her flashlight and hop-scotched past him, making him hold his breath between gasping. The worry wort. "She said it was in the back." She went directly to the farthest sheet-draped shape as if she already knew, and pulled the dusty sheet away.

Every inch of the wooden, oriental trunk was engraved. There were lions blowing windstorms on each corner of its flat top, and the bottom corners each sported what might be an owl, wings spread.

"This thing is gorgeous," she whispered, and she tried the brass hasp. It snapped open. "Unlocked."

Kneeling, she opened the lid, then pushed aside layers of newspaper before she realized it wasn't just there for padding. An old image, unmistakably Lady El, caught her eye, and she aimed her light and read the blurb about her performance at The Pink Flamingo. Then she checked the other newspapers. "They're all about her," she said, handing them to Jack, who had made his way across the attic more slowly than she had.

She handed him the rest, and leaned over the open trunk. A stack of record albums filled one side. The other side had a pile of books. Looked like old datebooks.

She took out the albums, one after another. The covers were all Lady El, and most of them much younger than she had appeared in the mirror. Lady El holding a fluffy Pomeranian under her chin, draped in blue silk. Lady El done up like Cleopatra, reclining on a fainting couch. Lady El in sequins, in velvet, in black satin, stroking a white cat. And that last one with a Lady El who was obviously far older, but every bit as sassy, in the same piano pose as one of the early ones.

"Those are pristine. They're worth a small fortune," Jack said.

"I will never part with these." She put the albums back with care and reached for the topmost book. It had 1965 on the cover and she opened it up, flipping through until she found the first page with an appointment written down. Then she frowned, "Jack, Jack, listen to this. 'Seance - 7 p.m. John and Mary C, whose son passed. Three-hundred-fifty dollars.'"

She rose and turned around to face him so she could see his reactions as she flipped to the next page. "'Seance. 8:30 p.m. Edna H, recently widowed. Three-hundred dollars.' And here. 'Seance, 10 a.m. Sam D'Voe. Three-hundred dollars. Introduce to Edna H.'" She flipped more pages and just kept finding more of the same. "Lady El *was* more than just a singer," she said. "I think she was a medium."

Turning back to the box, she picked out every datebook. There were five years' worth spanning from '65 to '69, the year Lady El had passed. She took them all out, and found, at the bottom of the pile, a hatbox. Its body was dusky rose, its lid mauve, and it had a satiny twisted rope handle of chocolate brown. She closed the trunk and sat on top of it, with the hatbox on her lap.

"This is it. She said I could use whatever I wanted, so I knew there would be something...usable in some way."

Jack came closer, crouching near. She took off the lid.

There was a black silk scarf, and beneath it, items wrapped in scarves of other colors. A deck of tarot cards was wrapped in a purple one. They had no box, just a ribbon tied around them. Their backs bore angels.

She handed the cards to Jack.

"I thought I knew all the decks, but I've never seen this one before," he said. He started to go through them card by card, as Kiley took out the silver-wrapped item and unwrapped it to reveal a round, slightly concave black mirror.

"Keep that covered," Jack advised. "You only expose scrying mirrors to moonlight or candlelight."

"Good tip." She wrapped the mirror and replaced it in the box.

The red scarf held a very large onyx pendulum, four inches long, on a string of amber and onyx beads. The green scarf held the oddest thing she'd ever seen. A mosaic eye, made out of thinly sliced gemstones in a silver frame. The retina was lapis lazuli, the pupil, obsidian, the white, milky quartz.

"What is this thing?" she asked.

"I don't know. Maybe Maya will."

Kiley put everything back into the hatbox and picked it up. "Will you bring down the albums?"

"I'll get them. Datebooks too," he said. She moved into his place and he moved into hers, opening the trunk to take the stack of albums out. There were seven of them. He piled datebooks on top, and closed the trunk with his foot. "And in one trip, no less."

"Trip being the operative word. Be careful, babe."

"Don't worry. I'm not ready to be a ghost yet."

Kiley led the way back to the doorway, noticing how there was a turret up overhead, but no way to get up into it. "Next time we come up here, we bring a ladder," she said as they moved beneath its trapdoor.

"Deal," he said. "This is amazing space up here."

"This whole place is amazing. I knew it the minute I first saw it, it's just…special."

He stopped following her, she realized when she got to the doorway and looked back. "What?"

"It's the house."

"Yes, it's a house. Wait, what's the house?"

"That's why you connect to Lady El and the rest of us don't. You connect to this house on such a deep level. And she's the soul of the house, you said."

"*She* said." Then she frowned. "You think that's it?"

He shrugged. "It's a theory. Open the door, this stuff's getting heavy."

CHAPTER TWENTY

"I miss my own place," Maya said.

She and Johnny had brought his grandfather's journals out onto the front porch, and were going through them alone. He liked it that way. The others were all doing equally important things in between ghostly outbursts.

"I haven't even settled into my own place yet."

"Jack's cabin is a great space. You should let me help you decorate."

He returned his gaze to the volume in his hand because they both knew that wouldn't go well. Not if keeping out of each other's arms was the goal.

"The gang are all pretty tight with my grandfather, yes?"

"I think Jack and I are the closest," she said. "Chris and Kiley only met him when he came in to help with that first big case. But I've worked with John, gosh, a dozen times over the past five years or so."

"Worked with him how?" he asked, noticing how good the breeze felt, how warm.

"Healing rites, mostly. That's his thing. No need for a shop or location; he makes appointments by phone and goes to the patient. I'd do my thing and he'd do his, and–"

"What's his thing?" he asked. "What does he do, exactly?"

"He sings."

"Just…sings?"

She nodded. "And keeps time with a rattle, and maybe burns some herbs and wafts the smoke over the person. It's not so much what he does, as the feeling of it. The energy of it. It's beautiful to be present when he works. Took my breath away every time, really, the connection he has is like a physical presence."

Johnny had never seen that for himself. He wished he had with everything in him and hoped he would still have the chance. And then he said, "And what's your thing? What were you doing while he was doing all that?"

"Directing Source energy through my hands and into the patient to help restore energetic balance." She held her hands in front of her with her thumbs touching, to show him how.

"I wish I'd been there. I'm really glad you were, though."

"I'm glad, too," she said. "And maybe someday soon all three of us can work together like that."

"That would be amazing."

The neighborhood was looking better. Crews had removed the broken pavement and filled the space with a temporary surface of compacted stone that crunched under tires. The brand new telephone pole was lighter brown than all the others. The power was back on. All in all, they'd done a good job cleaning up. There were loose branches on the lawn, but like everyone else on the block, they'd taken precautions. No lawn furniture or garbage cans had been left out, and all the limbs and refuse were secured. So the ghosts could rage-storm their hearts out, it wasn't going to do much more damage, though he supposed they could try to snap that rookie pole.

"Thanks for going with me this morning. I wouldn't have wanted to have been alone."

She took a deep breath and almost put her hand on his shoulder, then pulled it back. "This is harder than I thought it would be."

"Glad to know I'm not the only one."

A door closed somewhere inside. There were footsteps and muted voices.

"I think we need more help with this," Maya said.

"Yeah, I agree." He got up and she did, too. They went inside together. "Hey, everyone?" he called.

They came from various directions into the living room.

"You found anything in the journals yet?" Jack asked.

"We've found a lot of things. Those books are treasures," Maya said, "But I think we need everyone's help on this if we're going to find the specific thing we need. Especially since we don't know what we're looking for."

"I just hope what we need is in one of them," Johnny said." He set the box on the coffee table, and starting to hand around the volumes, beginning with those he and Maya had already perused, in case they'd missed anything. "How long before we can expect the next rage storm?"

"An hour at least," Breia said. She took a book and found a chair near Ryan, who sat on the hearth with his volume. "But it's hard to say. They're not regular anymore. Haven't been the last few times."

"I've noticed that, too," Maya said.

Kiley sat on the sofa beside Jack. "Our house ghost, Lady El says somebody they love who has very recently passed, might be able to lead them across. Something about the light inside them having to be rekindled. Apparently, reuniting with somebody they love would do that. Granted, that's not much help, unless somebody they cared about died in the last day or so."

"They don't love anybody but each other," Breia said.

"And us," Ryan added.

His sister's lips pulled into grimace. "That's not love. But they probably think it is."

Johnny nodded. "My grandfather said something in his journals would help, so let's find it." He untied the lace of the volume he'd taken from the bottom of the box, and opened it.

"'I was seventeen the first time I knew I could heal,'" he read aloud, automatically seeking Maya. They were the only two still standing up. He found her eyes, blue as sapphires, gazing right back. She knew how much these journals meant to him. She knew that his grandfather wanting him to have them, meant even more. She might be the only person who knew.

He was flipping pages while caught in Maya's eyes, and something fell out of the book, but he moved one hand fast and caught it before it hit the floor.

"Reflexes like a cat," Chris said in sportcaster-voice. "What is it?"

"It's a choker," Maya said.

Lying flat across his palm, draping over both sides, was a beaded neck band about two inches wide. It had a white beaded background with a multicolored diamond pattern all the way around in red, blue and yellow. Each diamond held a symbol. A spider. Wavy lines. The Sun. Other shapes he couldn't put a name to and would have to interpret later. It narrowed to a point on each end, with long strands dangling from both. Setting the journal down, Johnny ran his fingertips over the cool, smooth beads. The blue ones were turquoise, but he wasn't sure about the rest of them.

The others were flipping pages, skimming lines of his grandfather's handwriting, a mostly upright combination of print and cursive. They were glancing his way occasionally, curious about the necklace but otherwise, focused on finding something in the journals that would help.

Not Maya, though. Maya was riveted to him, and she moved a couple steps nearer where he stood.

Taking the choker by each string, Johnny tied it around his neck. He felt something rush through him that made him close his eyes. Imagination? Nostalgia? Maybe it was his grandfather's energy still clinging to the beads. Maybe it was something more. He felt a tingle in every nerve ending and knew, without any doubt, he'd found what they needed.

"You can stop looking," he told the others, his first two fingers touching the beaded treasure that encircled his neck. "This is what he wanted me to find. Thank you, Grandfather. Wherever you are."

"What is it? What does it do?" Kiley asked, getting up and moving closer.

"I don't know," Johnny said.

"Okay, well, if it's what we need, it's what we need. I have a few goodies of my own to add to our arsenal." Kiley dropped her journal into the box on the coffee table and headed into the dining room. Everyone else followed suit.

There was an old hat box on the dining room table. "Lady El was a medium," she said. "There's a trunk in the attic that was full of her datebooks, and she held seances here all the time."

"And made bank off it, too," Jack added.

"No wonder this place is so ghost-friendly," Chris said. "I knew there was a reason."

"She said I could use what I found there," Kiley said. "And the only other stuff in the trunk, besides a stack of her albums—"

"Her albums?" Chris asked, almost bouncing up and down.

"Yes, her albums. We'll play them later." She glanced at empty space and said, "You have a true fan, here Lady El."

"Sorry to get off topic," Chris said. "The only other stuff in the trunk is in that hatbox, yes?"

"Yes."

Kiley opened the hatbox and took out the items, one by one. A black mirror, an dark gemstone pendulum, a deck of cards, and an inlaid mosaic eye about six inches long.

"The only person we know they loved, who is also dead, is Benji," Kiley said. "I think we need to try again to get his help."

"We tried before and it didn't go so well," Ryan pointed out.

"But now we have Lady El's eye and John Redhawk's beads," Maya said. "And we're clearer on the goal. We have to show them something that will light them up."

Johnny nodded. "And what's going to light them up more than reuniting with the baby they lost? We need Benji's help. We have no choice. We have to try again."

164

CHAPTER TWENTY-ONE

here hadn't been a storm in ninety-seven minutes when Kiley took her seat at the dining room table. "I wonder what's taking them so long?"

The plan was to begin the seance immediately after the next attack in hopes the dead would be too tired to try to possess the living. But the expected attack had not yet come.

"Let's just do it," Breia said. "Let's get it over with." She sat at the head of the table, and her brother at the foot.

Maya was moving around the gathered group as the others found seats. She was passing out silver spoons and iron nails. "Hold one in each palm when you join hands. Iron to iron, silver to silver."

They looked at each other, muttering and switching the items from one hand to the other until they had it right.

She had already made a circle of water around the entire room. Every pitcher, glass, and bowlful was in contact with the one beside it. They lined the walls along the mopboard trim, and crossed every threshold.

"I agree, we should go ahead," Kiley said.

Ryan nodded. "Let's talk to my big brother, Benji."

So, they joined hands, awkwardly pressing their nails and spoons together.

Maya took her seat and spoke. "Spirits of light, come ye that may. Keep the darkness ever at bay."

Then Kiley ad libbed, "Lady El, help us out here, if you can. Help the troubled spirits of Robert and Mindi find peace and release."

Yeah, I'll help you kick their sorry asses out.

Kiley popped her eyes open and looked around the room. In the mirror atop the buffet, Lady El wore a sarcastic expression and what looked like a diamond studded headband.

She wanted to reply but didn't want to talk out loud and disrupt the energy or whatever. So she tried thinking her words. *What does that eye thing do? How do we use it?*

Damned if I know. I never figured it out when I was alive. Guess we'll know when we need to know.

How can you be so sure of that?

What, toots, you haven't figured it out yet? That's how things work.

"Grandfather," Johnny said, "If you can feel me, if you can send your energy from wherever you are, please help us as we guide the spirits of Robert and Mindi to peace where they belong. Combine your powers with ours," he put his hand on the choker, "and help us to summon Benji, their son, to convince them to cross."

Kiley watched his face, but she couldn't tell if he heard a reply or not. She hoped John was there with them, somehow, even though he might be far away. He'd certainly proven the power of his connection to them, or to Johnny, or both. She looked around the room but didn't see any indication one way or another. So she just beamed love from her heart for him and imagined that wherever he was, John must feel it.

Finally, Jack got his turn. "Benji Sousa, we summon, stir, and call you forth. We need your help. Your mother and your father need your help. Come to them, Benji. Show them the way. They need you to convince them to cross over."

There was an odd hum and Kiley opened her eyes. The whole room was bathed in a kind of soft orange light. It was everywhere, as if the very air was lit with it.

Jack's head fell backward, his eyes opened, backlit with that same ethereal glow. He said, "I am light." His voice was soft, not like his own. Almost like he might've sounded as a youngster. "They can't see me, they can't *bear* me. They are dark. So dark."

"Seeing you would bring them some light, though," Kiley said. "Wouldn't it?"

"They couldn't bear this brightness from their darkness. Do you understand?"

"The energy's too different." Maya said. "The vibrations are too far apart."

"You do understand. They cannot see me now. I am invisible to them. They see only darkness, frustration and pain."

"So how do we get a couple of dark, tormented souls to experience a moment of light so they can find their way across?" Kiley asked.

But there was no answer. Jack brought his head level, blinking as if to clear a haze from his eyes. Outside, the wind moaned a warning.

"He's done," Kiley said. "Wrap it up, Maya."

Maya spoke quickly but clearly. "Friendly spirit, speak no more. Now I close the western door. Turn the lock that has no key. Portal close. So mote it be." Then louder, "The circle is open."

They all relaxed their hands, and then something hit the side of the house so hard they all jumped and one or two squeaked in alarm. A window shattered. Breia screamed and threw herself out of her chair into Johnny's arms. He wrapped one arm around her and as he got up, reached out to pull Ryan into their huddle.

Maya was on her feet, too. She raised her arms over her head and began chanting in some other language.

Kiley said, "Lady El! What can we do to give them a spark of light?"

I don't know. Give 'em one of their freaking kids?

"Not an option. We're not giving them the kids."

I don't think they're asking. You shouldn't have opened the door.

Jack, who was still in his chair, said, "Talk to me, Robert and Mindi! Talk to me so I can help you get what you need to move on!" He spread his arms wide, opened his hand and let the silver spoon and coffin nail fall to the polished wood table.

"Jack, what are you *doing*?" Kiley lunged toward the big dumbass, but before she got there, he threw his head backward so hard his chair went over, and then he lay there on the floor.

She fell to her knees beside him, and said, "Lady El, if you can help, you'd better damn well help, or I swear I'll have this place leveled."

The wind outside intensified. The house began to shake, and Johnny wondered if Kiley's threat would be carried out by the ghosts themselves. The whole place was trembling, the windows rattling in their frames. He kept one arm around Breia and the other around Ryan, as if he could protect them.

Another window broke and the wind rushed inside. Magazines and mail danced and swirled.

"Get them out of here!" Kiley shouted.

She had to shout or he wouldn't have heard her over the howling. He turned and hustled Breia and Ryan across the living room, toward the stairway, but then he heard glass breaking upstairs, so he turned back the other way.

Jack was trying to get up off the floor, and Kiley was trying to hold him down. Maya and Chris tried to help her, but Jack threw everybody off him. Kiley stumbled backward, hit her head on the dining table, and cussed him out royally. Jack came up furious and surged right past her, heading straight at Johnny.

"You can't keep my son from me!" he roared. His voice wasn't human but something deeper that echoed as if from the pits of hell. His eyes were black holes, swirling ink backlit with something awful. Hate. Rage.

Breia pried herself out of Johnny's arms, lunged at Jack and smacked him across the face hard enough to leave a mark while the maelstrom raged around them all. "What about your daughter, Dad! What about me? Why aren't you tearing the world apart trying to get to me?"

"You do not need us. You are strong."

"So is Ryan!" she cried. "But you're ruining his life! Both our lives!"

"We have to protect–"

"You left Benji and he died. Now you've abandoned him again." She gestured at empty space with her arms. "He waits for his parents on the other side, but his parents refuse to go."

"Benji is lost to us."

"You're the ones who are lost to him! He's in the light, but you live in darkness. This isn't where you belong. Your pain will only end if you let go. Go so that I can love you again. Because you have made me hate you."

"You've made us both hate you." Ryan said the words so passionately he spat them. "We hate you. We hate you. We–"

Kiley said, "Ryan, I don't think that's the best way to…"

The roaring wind let up and the air went still and suddenly heavy. Johnny felt the weight of it on his back. On all their backs.

"Our children hate us," the thing inside Jack said.

"I don't want to hate you." Breia moved closer. "I want you to feel joy again. I want the light inside you to re-ignite, so you can let go of your rage and your pain. Let go of Ryan."

"Let go of this world," Maya said softly.

She'd been inching closer to Breia the whole time.

"Let go of this world," Breia repeated. "Let go and move on. Go find Benji. Go find peace."

Maya moved closer. "Shed your anger. Shed your pain. Rise from it."

"Rise from it," Breia said. "Let me help you."

Jack who wasn't Jack, reached a hand toward her, and Breia, nodding her head slowly, reached out and touched her fingertips to his and whispered, "Don't take Ryan. Take me instead."

Jack grabbed her wrist, and then he slumped to the floor, but the dark thing that had been inside him still had hold of Briea's wrist. And she wasn't even struggling.

Johnny grabbed her arm and tried to pull her free. "Let her go!"

But the shadow jerked her upward so powerfully it seemed her arm would tear from her body. Her head smashed into the ceiling and her body crashed back down to the floor.

Ryan screamed his sister's name, flinging himself onto the floor beside her. But Johnny saw her rising up out of her body, a translucent shadow of herself. It made no sense that he could see her. He did not see the dead.

She looked around as if confused.

"Oh, no," he whispered. "Oh, no, Breia, no."

She smiled at him, but then noticed her body on the floor and seemed to understand all at once. The shock hit her and he felt it too, like a wave of energy surging in his chest, speeding up his heart.

"Oh," she said. "It worked." Her gaze was drawn to something in the distance. And then she looked back, first at Johnny, and then at Ryan. It was then he realized everyone else in the room had frozen in time. Nobody was moving.

"You've gotta take care of my brother," Breia said.

"I don't think you're hurt that bad. I'll do CPR. Why don't you try to get back in your body?"

She looked away from him at nothing he could see. "Because I can fix this. I'm the only one who can. Look, they see me. Oh my gosh, they're lighting up. It's happening."

"I can't see anything but you," he said.

She didn't look back at him, though he wished she would. "I know the way. It's right there, I see it. I can make them see it, too."

"Just point them in the right direction and get back in your body, okay?"

"I don't think it works that way."

"Try, Breia. You have to try. Ryan needs you." As he spoke, he pressed his hand to his neck and his palm covered his grandfather's beads. It felt as if he'd grabbed a live wire. A jolt rocketed through him and the world launched into motion again. "No," he said, looking around. "No!"

Kiley was helping Jack get up onto his feet. He blinked like he didn't know where he was. Breia's body was still on the floor. He went to her, knelt beside her opposite her brother. "Breia, come back. Come on. Come back."

"She's not breathing," Ryan said. "Do something!"

Johnny tilted up her chin and lay his head on her chest, but he already knew he would hear no heartbeat. There was no more time to wait.

He straightened up above her and gave her one breath, then another. Then he positioned his hands over her chest and began compressions.

"I thought they eliminated the breaths," Kiley said. "Don't you just do compressions now?" She had her phone in her hand and was tapping. The storm had silenced.

Chris said, "Actually, they eliminated the breaths because people are more likely to render aid if it doesn't involve mouth-to-mouth, so overall survival rate goes up."

"People are assholes," Kiley said. Then she moved a step away and spoke to the 911 dispatcher on the phone.

Johnny looked up, not sure why, and saw his grandfather standing with the others. He was not young as he had been when

Johnny had visited him in the past. He was just as he had been the last time they'd been together. He was not smiling, but he wore a serene expression and he met Johnny's eyes, and very deliberately, he put his hand on his neck. Johnny saw that his grandfather wore the very beaded necklace that he was wearing himself. The old man nodded. Johnny stopped pushing on Breia's chest, and pressed his hand to his own necklace in exactly the same way.

Chris said, "I got this," and took over the chest compressions.

Grandfather closed his eyes, and so Johnny did, too, and yet could still see everything.

The room had gone hazy and kind of wavery, and it was all bathed in that orange glow. Everyone had frozen in time again. Kiley was on the phone, but staring nervously toward the windows. A woman in a red-sequined gown with a long cigarette holder, who had to be Lady El, was reflected in the window glass, but was not frozen. She was yelling at Kiley, *Use the eye! Use the damned eye!* But Kiley was paralyzed in time so Johnny didn't know if she heard.

Jack was behind Chris, who was poised with his hands over Breia's sternum. Ryan knelt on the other side of her with his head in his hands. Maya … Maya was gazing right into his eyes, and yet as frozen in time as everyone else.

His grandfather was standing beside him, and he said, "The parents lit up as soon as the daughter was with them again. And now they can see the boy on the other side. Look." He raised an arm, pointing toward the wall, but it wasn't a wall anymore. It had become a meadow of wildflowers all the way to a distant horizon. There was a path through the blossoms that vanished into sky. He detected a hint of that orange glow where it ended.

I told you to give them one of their kids. Lady El puffed her smoke. *Worked like a charm.*

Johnny didn't even look her way. Breia was walking away from him on that path, her form less solid than before, but glowing with light. On either side of her, there were oblong shapes of gray mist, and they gave the impression of holding her hands. Her parents, clearly.

Breia was moving in ultra-slow-motion toward where the path vanished into that orange-ish light. Not orange, exactly. Not any color he'd ever seen before. His brain wanted to call it an orange but that's not what it was. He walked toward her and he, too, moved in extended, warped time.

With each step she took, Breia glowed brighter, and the gray blobs beside her lightened in successive, minuscule shades and the light within them seemed to grow brighter.

Dammit, Kiley, use the mother fucking eye, Lady El shouted.

Johnny strained to move faster, reached out for Breia, but he couldn't get to her in time. He couldn't do it. He *couldn't*…

He snapped back so suddenly he felt a physical whiplash effect. He had to shake his head to set himself back in real time and space. The people around him came to life.

"Come on," Chris said, pumping. "Come on, Breia!"

"Come on Breia. Come back," Ryan said, and then he said it again, and then the others all joined in shouting and yelling. Maya came to stand where Johnny was standing. She put her hands on his shoulders, gazed into his eyes, and then closed hers and whispered, "Come back, Breia. Come back."

Johnny put his hand on his neck band. "Come back, Breia. Come back."

Kiley jerked her head around like she'd heard something, lunged for the dining table, grabbed the mosaic eye and whipped it against the fireplace. It smashed to bits. There was a flash of that weird light that filled the entire room and everyone fell into stunned silence.

Then Breia dragged in a loud, high-pitched breath.

Chris straightened away from her chest, startled. And then he just laughed. "I did it! Holy shit, I did it!"

"Yeah, you did it all right." Kiley was smiling into Jack's eyes as she said it.

Jack smacked Chris on the back and said. "Good job, kid."

Still kneeling, Ryan pulled his big sister Breia upright and into his arms. "Jeeze, I thought I lost you."

"Oh, God, I'm back," she whispered in a voice that didn't match the excitement and joy the rest of them were feeling. "I'm back. I didn't think..." She groaned a little, pressed the heel of one hand to her forehead, and lay back down, right on the floor where she was. "I need a minute."

"Um, guys?" Jack nodded toward the fireplace and Johnny looked that way.

Pieces of the thing Kiley had smashed were vanishing one by one. Like they were just blinking out.

"That's the eye," Kiley said.

"I know," Johnny said. "I saw Lady El for a minute. She was yelling at you to use it."

"You saw her?" Kiley asked. "Isn't she amazing?"

"She is," he agreed.

Maya was looking toward Breia, who was still lying on the floor, as if she were worried about her. She went to hover over her the way Chris and Ryan still were.

"Lady El told you to use the eye?" Jack asked.

Kiley nodded.

"So naturally, you smashed it to smithereens," he said.

"Naturally," she replied, deadpan. Then she shrugged. "I don't know what made me throw it. But I guess it's served its purpose and now it's fading away or... OhmyGod it's in my hand." She opened her hand and there it was, lying across her palm, extending past either side, perfectly intact. She high-stepped to the table, holding the eye as far from her as she could, and slid the thing back into its hatbox. Then put on the lid. "Eeeesh!" She wiped her palm on her pant leg.

Johnny saw Breia get up at last, and she walked away from her brother and Chris and Maya, who were still kneeling on the floor, and came to Johnny, who stood a few steps away. "Wow," she said.

"Thank God you're okay," he replied. "Do you know what happened? Do you remember it?"

"I remember everything. I took them through," she said. "I was right there. God, it was so beautiful. There's this light that you can touch. It permeates you, and feels... good beyond description. So good."

"You went through?"

"Johnny," Maya called. But he waved a hand at her, and kept listening to Breia.

"I held their hands and walked them through," she went on. "And they just lit up. I mean, they were them again, you know? They were Mom and Dad again. And Benji was there waiting. They ran to him and the light was filling me, and I tried to follow. But something pulled me back."

She looked down at the floor, then up at Johnny. "I saw your grandfather. At least I felt like that's who it was. He was on this side of the gate, but he waved as I passed, and I felt his love for you swelling inside him." She blinked away tears, took a breath, seemed to steady herself. "And then I was back in my body, and I– Oh. My body." She was looking toward where the others knelt.

"Johnny!" Maya said. "Who the hell are you talking to? Get over here, she's passed out again."

He looked toward Kiley and saw Breia on the floor, right where she'd fallen, then looked beside him, but Breia wasn't there. She'd never got up and walked over to him. Or maybe only a part of her had.

Breia, on the floor, moaned and open her eyes. She came around slowly, and the others helped her sit up. She kept touching her forearms and hands. And then she looked at Johnny, met his eyes, and he knew that he hadn't imagined the conversation they had just had. He didn't know how it had happened or what it meant, but Breia had left her body just then.

"I took our parents across," Breia said. They all helped her to her feet, and into the living room to the sofa. Jack came behind them with an ice pack for her head, which she took gratefully. "Something pulled me back."

"I think we all pulled you back," Johnny said. He touched his necklace, saw Kiley looking back into the dining room at the hat box that held the eye. He recalled them all calling Breia to return while Chris had kept her body alive to receive her.

"That's exactly what happened," Breia said. She had tears brimming in her eyes. "Ryan, honey, they said to tell you they're sorry. They lost their minds at the thought of leaving another son behind. They hope you can forgive them."

Ryan hugged his sister. "You died to protect me, Breia. Man, I can't believe you did that. And if you ever do it again I'll kill you."

CHAPTER TWENTY-TWO

"So," Johnny said, because what else was he supposed to say? Everyone had gone home, to their own, actual homes. He imagined Jack and Kiley would be as happy about that as any of them. He couldn't wait to get to his own place. He had a lot to process.

He'd driven Breia and Ryan, because they'd left their car at their place. The gas had all been aired out of their cute little house and it was deemed safe for occupancy according to the letter left on the door by the local FD.

Ryan said he was going to hit the shower and his bed, in that order, and headed upstairs.

Breia and Johnny sat down on the front porch, top step, sipping bottled iced tea. He said, "So… you left your body for a few seconds back there, yeah?"

"After I came back into it."

"Right, from the dead."

"Not dead," she said. "There was nothing dead about that."

"I think I was the only one who could see you."

Breia nodded and pushed her hair behind her ear on one side. "It seemed that way, yes."

MAGGIE SHAYNE

"And then when you looked back and noticed your body lying there on the floor..." He stopped and nodded at her.

"I popped right back in."

"How?" he asked.

She lifted the bottle of tea to her lips. "It was like I thought, I should get back in my body, and then I moved toward it, just took a step in that direction, and *zap*. I'm blinking open my own eyes again, which, by the way, are nowhere near as clear and focused as my other set."

"Your other set?"

"When I'm not in my body."

He nodded, considering all that. "Do you know if it was a one-time thing, or whether you can get out of your body again? You know. At will?"

She took another sip. Apparently, death and resurrection left you thirsty. "I'm kind of scared to try, to be honest. What if I can get out, but then can't figure out how to get back in?"

"You just decide to get back in, and take a step toward your body. Right?"

"I... guess."

"So?"

She closed her eyes, took a deep nasal breath. Johnny watched her closely but nothing happened.

After a second, she opened her eyes and shrugged. "Guess not."

"Guess not," he said. "Are you all right? You going to be able to sleep?"

"They're gone. We're safe, for the first time in a long time. Yes, I'll sleep like the... " She bit her lip, lowered her head, didn't finish the sentence. "I'll sleep." She looked up at him again.

"Okay."

"Thanks for bringing us home, Johnny. And... for saving our lives. For everything."

"It's what we do."

178

She nodded, looked away for a second. "When I said my vision was clearer out of my body, I didn't just mean my eyesight. You're in love with Maya."

He blinked in shock at the blunt statement that felt like it hit him between the eyes. "I don't... I mean, I don't think I—"

"You love her. And that's okay with me. I mean, I thought we had some chemistry, you and me, but it's beautiful, what's between you two." She squeezed his arm. "She's your destiny. That's kind of huge." Then she let go. "I'm happy for you and not at all sad for myself. Life is too precious to spend it on sadness. I know that more than I ever did before." She flashed a dazzling smile. "Besides, I saw my future love, my perfect soulmate and he is amazing."

"Wow. That's... great. I'm glad for you."

"Me, too. I wonder when he's going to show up."

Johnny got to his feet, reeling from what she'd told him. Did he love Maya? If she was his destiny, what did that mean? Did it mean they were inevitable, or that if they missed out on each other, neither would ever be fulfilled with anyone else? And what about her? How did Maya really feel about him? He wanted to ask Breia if she'd picked up an inkling about that mystery from the other side, but decided that if she had, she'd have said so.

She was looking at him now, her short dark hair tousled, her brown eyes wide and pretty and somehow deeper than they'd seemed before, waiting for him to say something. "Um, I'm gonna head home, if you guys are okay here."

"We're okay here. Thanks to you and the gang. Bye, Johnny."

He started down the steps to his truck. Then he stopped and turned around. "Don't be a stranger. Come around now and then."

"You, too," she said. "All of you." Then her smile froze, turned into a frown, and she added, "I'm supposed to tell you that the janitor didn't die the way they say he did." Then she waved good-bye, got up and went inside.

Johnny expelled a long breath as he pulled to a stop at his cabin. Nice. He'd finally thought of it that way automatically. *His* cabin. He sat there and admired its simple, ranch-style, L-shaped design. The front door was green. He wondered if that had some sort of spiritual meaning for Jack, or if just happened to be green, and made a mental note to ask. But for now, he just wanted to be alone.

He got out of his truck and went inside, and the first thing he did was build a fire in the fireplace. He needed cozy, tonight. He had a lot to process.

While the fire took off, he hit the shower for a brief, steaming hot session. He'd have savored it longer if not for the fact that he could barely keep his eyes open.

He toweled off, pulled on fresh shorts and a robe, brushed his teeth, and headed straight for the world's softest sofa right in front of the fire. Stretching out on it, he pulled the fake fur throw off the back and over him and closed his eyes.

Knock knock knock.

"No," he said.

"It's Maya. I only need a minute."

"*Yes.*" He only whispered that part. He got up onto his feet and pulled his robe around him on his way to open the door.

Maya blinked and stared at his chest and said, "Holy shit."

"Sorry. I was…I just got out of the shower, and… Come on in." He reached to tie the robe, like auto-pilot, and then decided to let it be.

"It won't take long," she said, moving a little bit farther into his cabin. Not far enough. "I just… There's something I want to tell you, Johnny."

"There's something I want to tell you, too," he said. Because he'd been mulling on it, and he was pretty sure Breia was right.

He loved her. And if they were meant to be, they might as well get on with it, right?

"I know," Maya said. "You and Breia, I know. I'm happy for you–"

"No."

"—that's partly why I—"

He kissed her. He just stepped closer, leaned in and kissed her. And when she didn't slap his face, he wrapped his arms around her and held her close kept on kissing her.

She was wrapped around him too, one hand pressed to his back, one in his hair. She kissed him back, and finally tapped out, turning her head away, breathing fast.

"Partly why you what?" he asked. And when she looked blank, "You said, 'that's partly why I…'"

She backed up a step, smoothed her hair, shook her head. "Why I started dating my ex again," she said, finally looking at him. But she couldn't hold his eyes for long.

Everything in Johnny's brain ground to a halt, causing a three-hundred-thought pileup. "You *what*, now?"

"Joe. We've been texting, and he's all alone, and we always had a good time together. I mean it's not serious, I just feel like… I feel like you need space from me, so you can really explore—"

"You know what I need more than I do, then." He nodded and thought he was bobbing his head way too much as he reached past her for the door, opened it, and willed her to leave with every fiber of his being. "Thanks for letting me know," he said. "All the best to you and Jeff."

"Joe."

"Don't care. Please leave."

She blinked at him. "Johnny?"

"I'm exhausted, Maya. I don't need an update on your love life, I need twelve solid hours of sleep." He looked pointedly through the door he was holding open.

"Oh. Well, me too. Yeah. Okay. I just… Okay." She walked out. "Good night, Johnny."

"Night." He swung the door closed, leaned against it, and felt a darkness creeping over his soul.

"Don't let it get to you."

He lifted his head from his folded arms to see Breia standing behind him in a long white nightgown or dress or something, and he quickly tied up his robe. "How the hell did you get in?" He looked past her toward the back door. "What is going on, have I got a flashing neon visitors-wanted sign somewhere I don't know about?"

She laughed like she didn't have a clue what he was talking about and also like it didn't matter, because she had something on her mind. "Yeah, here's the thing," she said. "I um…I think I need your help. Professionally, I mean. Because, I'm at home lying in my bed right now, and something pulled me right out of my body and all the way to a spot about a mile up your road. And here I am. And I don't know why, and I'm not sure I can find my way back and this is just…"

She started to cry.

Johnny went over to offer a hug, and she felt real to him. It was the oddest thing. And then her back kind of moved under his hands in a way backs don't normally do, and he pulled away, startled.

"Yeah, also, there's that."

"There's what?" He backed two more steps from her to try and figure out what the hell was happening.

She sighed and a set of wings unfurled behind her. Not behind her, *from* her.

"You have wings."

"Yeah. They're kind of … well, would you call them angelic?"

He nodded. "I would, in fact, call them angelic. Yes, that's exactly how I'd describe them." He checked for a halo. "Holy shit, there's a nimbus of light around you."

"Yeah."

"I feel like I should bow or something."

She shrugged. "I'd settle for a ride back to my place."

A completely inappropriate laugh bubbled out of him and he bit it back, but then it emerged again, fully this time. He covered his mouth and still it escaped. When he could catch his breath, he said, "I'm sorry, really, it's just... You have wings and you need a ride."

"I know. I know, believe me I know. I'm just afraid I'll get lost if I try to get home by myself. Everything looks different from here."

"Of course I'll drive you home," he said. I'm happy to drive you home. Come on, come on in. Let me throw on some clothes and get you into the truck."

She folded her wings and they vanished. He got into fresh jeans and a shirt, grabbed a hoodie and walked her out to the truck, then pulled out to drive back up the long and winding gravel road toward town. They passed the spot where he'd first met Ryan, and Johnny thought about the wild journey they'd taken since. He felt good about what he did. He and the gang. They helped people.

He saw another set of headlights coming toward them from the distance.

Breia yelled, "Stop!" so suddenly he hit the brakes, thinking something had run out in front of them. She wrenched open her door and jumped out of the truck. "This is where I'm supposed to be. Right here."

"Okay. Okay." He pulled the truck off onto the shoulder, door still hanging wide, and shut the headlights off so they wouldn't blind the oncoming driver. He left the running lights on to keep his truck visible. Then he got out and went to stand with Breia alongside the gravel road. She was staring at the oncoming vehicle.

"Do you know who that is?" Johnny asked.

"No."

The car was moving slowly. It came nearer, and then slowed even more until the road curved and the car didn't. It kept going straight, rolling off the side of the road directly across from where he and Breia stood. It came to a gentle stop when it bumped a tree stump.

Johnny and Breia ran across the road. Johnny got there first and saw a woman with silver curls slumped over her steering wheel. He opened the door and reached in to feel her neck in search of a pulse. "Are you all right? Ma'am, are you okay?"

"She's okay," Briea said.

He glanced over his shoulder to see her standing behind him with her hand out to the side in an odd way. She smiled at him, reaching her other hand toward him. "I know why I'm here now." And she wiggled her fingers at him.

Johnny took her hand. As soon as he touched Breia, a woman appeared beside her. She had silver curls and Breia was holding her hand, too. The woman saw the car and the body inside, and said, "Am I dead?"

"You're perfectly alive," Breia told her. "There's no such thing as dead."

The woman looked around her and stopped on something in the distance, something Johnny couldn't see, and she breathed, "Oh my." And then her silver curls started to turn darker, and the wrinkles smoothed from her face. "Will you walk with me?"

"That's what I'm here for," Breia said. And then she squeezed Johnny's hand and said, "I have to go. But...will you wait?"

He nodded, kind of speechless.

Breia let go of his hand, and the old woman vanished. Breia's wings extended, and still holding the hand of the woman Johnny could no longer see, she flew away.

She freaking *flew away.*

~

Johnny was glad that it was only a fifteen-minute drive back to Breia and Ryan's house. She hadn't said much since she'd returned from her mission and her gaze was kind of inward, like she was processing it all.

He stopped in front of her house and she said, "Thanks again, Johnny. Seems like I'm always thanking you."

"That's what friends are for. I'll wait here until you're back in your body. So let me know when you are, okay?"

"Okay. And after that, I need help to figure all this out. I guess I need to re-hire you guys, if you think there's anything you can do."

"Hire us? Breia, has it occurred to you that you should be working with us?"

She frowned, tilting her head to one side. "I never thought about that."

"You crossed over. You came back with something extra, the ability to leave your body and sprout angel wings. You have an extra sense that draws you straight to people who are about to die so you can help them cross over."

"Is that what you think it is?"

"That's what it just was," he said.

She frowned. "So...am I some kind of ...death angel?" She clapped a hand over her mouth and around it, said, "Ohmygosh, am I the Grim Reaper?"

"Only if the Grim Reaper is Tinkerbell," he said. "You're not the grim anything. You helped that woman find her way. If you'd had this power when your parents died, you could have shown them the way, too, and prevented all this. You're a guide."

"You think?"

He nodded. "I do."

"Wow," she said. "Just ... wow."

"Before you go in, can I ask you something? It's going to sound pathetic and needy, but I need to know."

"I know you do, Johnny," she said, like she already knew his question. "And no, I didn't get any revelation about Maya's feelings the way I did about yours. But as a normal human woman, I've seen what's in her eyes when she looks at you, and so has Kiley. I've noticed her noticing. She's a total Jaya stan."

"Jaya?"

"Johnny, Maya. Jaya." She shrugged one shoulder. "Sleep on that. I'm gonna sleep on what you said, and we'll talk again, okay?" Then she waved her fingers and was gone. As in, she vanished. Didn't open the truck door or get out, just blinked away. Only two or three seconds ticked by before she appeared at her bedroom window in pajamas she hadn't been wearing before and gave him a thumbs-up.

"Well, what do you know about that?" he said. And then he headed home to get some sleep.

CHAPTER TWENTY-THREE

T he entire gang gathered with Breia and Ryan at the
cemetery where their parents and brother rested, on a
day in the newborn month of April, when the sun was so bright
and the sky so blue they didn't look real. It was sixty degrees with
a gentle south wind. The trees wore baby leaves of palest green.

Johnny hadn't told the gang about Breia's gifts. It was up to
her to tell them if and when she felt ready. But she'd invited them
all to a personal and private memorial for her parents, now that
they had finally crossed over. It was just the seven of them, gathered around the gravestone that seemed far less scary now than
the last time Johnny had been there. The gate and fence had
already been repaired.

He glanced at Jack, wondering if the guardians were still
surrounding the place, but he didn't want to interrupt the peace-
fulness of the moment to ask. Everyone had brought something,
an offering Maya said, but they were just gifts. His was a
climbing rose that he'd already planted behind the headstone so
it would grow up the back and creep around the front and sides.

"Let's begin," Breia said. She faced the gravestone, took a
watery breath. "Mom, Dad, I love you. And I vow to remember

who you were for the first ten years of my life, and who you were at the end when I held your hands once more. I'm not going to think of you, ever, as the beings you briefly became in between. And you need never worry about Ryan because I have him. I have him. And Benji, I wish I'd had the chance to know you, my brother, but I have a feeling I will someday."

She placed a wreath of flowers against the headstone, and looked at Ryan.

"Um. Okay. Thanks for giving me life, I guess. And for staying with me when I was a helpless preemie. And for trying to help me while I was growing up, but uh, I'm glad you're gone. Benji, I'm sorry we never met. Here's your bear." He tossed the ratty old teddy bear onto the grave in front of the wreath.

Jack said, "Go in peace," and put flowers on the grave.

Kiley said, "Don't come back," and put hers there.

Chris didn't say anything, just passed to Johnny with a look. Johnny didn't really have much to say to them either, but he muttered "Rest in peace," and turned to Maya.

Maya had a pouch of something that she scattered over the grave. It smelled incredible and looked like ground herbs with flower petals mixed in. Then she sang a gentle lyric. "Weaver, Weaver, weave their thread whole and strong into your web. Healer, Healer, heal their pain. In love may they return again."

And then they just stood in silence for a minute or two.

Jack, Kiley, Chris, and Maya were near the graveside, talking softly. Breia and Ryan came to where Johnny stood, a few feet away and hugged him.

Ryan said, "Thanks, dude. My life is so good now. I didn't know how not good it was until I was on this side of it, you know?"

"I do." He clasped Ryan's hand briefly, then the kid headed over to talk to Chris, giving him a private moment with Breia. "So how are you? And how is...you know, the thing?"

She shrugged. "I'm good. It's good seeing Ryan so happy."

188

"And?"

"And I think you were right about your theories. I've been called to take two more souls across since I last saw you, and it's only been two weeks. But I found my way back home both times. The first time, I thought I was lost and I panicked, but eventually I figured it out. The second time, I was able to close my eyes and picture my body and I just floated back to it. So that's the way."

"That's the way. You have any control over getting out of it yet?"

"No. It's spontaneous, but I think that's the point. I'm drawn to where I'm needed." She shrugged. "I just hope I don't, you know, pop out when I'm driving or anything."

"That wouldn't be great, would it? Well, you'll learn more about how it works as you go along, I guess."

"I think so, too."

A little commotion drew his attention, and they both turned. A tall scarecrow of a guy with brown hair and black framed glasses was ambling toward the gang at the graveside like he knew them. Maya hurried toward him and whisper-shouted, "I *told* I'd text you when I was finished here." She shot Johnny a glance and caught him looking.

The scarecrow had to be Joe. Her ex. Or ex-ex, to be more accurate.

"Oh my God," Breia said from beside Johnny in a tone of disbelief. "Oh. My. God. It's *you*!"

She launched so fast that for a second, Johnny thought she'd left her body again. But no, she was all in one piece as she sprinted past Maya and flung her arms around the tall dude's neck.

He reacted in shock, head back, eyes wide, mouth agape. But he was polite enough to put his hands on her waist to keep her from knocking them both flat on the ground.

Once he had his footing, he pulled her arms from around his neck as gently as Johnny figured a guy could and set her on the ground. He took a step back, looking at her the way one looks at a dog that might bite.

"Oh," Breia said. "Oh, gosh, I'm sorry. I guess... I'm sorry."

Clearly, she realized that everyone was looking at her as if she'd lost her marbles. Everyone but Johnny, who was feeling like a huge weight might be dissolving from his shoulders.

Breia took two more steps away from Scarecrow Joe, her cheeks flushing red. "I thought you were somebody else." Then she turned toward Johnny and lip synched *It's him*. Her smile and the delight in her eyes told him everything he needed to know. Maya's ex was Breia's soulmate.

Breia turned and grabbed Ryan by the hand. "Let's go, Ry."

Ryan gave a helpless shrug and went with her, but as they walked away, she kept looking back at Joe, who wore a perplexed expression but watched her go all the same.

Johnny took a deep breath and decided to man up. He walked over to Maya and Joe and extended a hand. "You must be Joe. I'm Johnny."

Joe shook and said, "I didn't mean to crash the, uh, funeral."

"I am really sorry about this, Johnny. I told him to stay away," Maya said.

Johnny wondered why she'd told him to stay away and figured it was because she didn't want it to seem like she was flaunting her old flame in his face. "It's fine."

"It's not. Come on, Joe." She took the guy by his elbow and propelled him across the grass toward the parking area, following the same path Breia and Ryan had taken.

Kiley said, "What the heck was that with Breia and Joe?"

"I don't know," Jack said. "Does she seem different to you?" he asked Johnny. "Lighter? I don't know why, but that seems like the only word for it. Lighter."

"She did come back different," Johnny said. "I imagine death changes a person in a lot of ways."

"Are you guys uh... you know?" Kiley asked. "Dating, or...?"

"No, no, that was one of the differences. She said she'd seen her future love and he was amazing." Did he sound a little smug when he said that?

They all looked toward the parking lot where Maya was talking a mile a minute at poor Joe as he folded his lanky frame into her small car.

Johnny crossed his arms and smiled. Kiley met his eyes and smiled right back.

Jack and Chris just looked at each other and shrugged.

**Continue Reading for an excerpt from
GIRL BLUE.**

NEW YORK TIMES BESTSELLING AUTHOR

MAGGIE SHAYNE

A Brown and de Luca Novel

GIRL BLUE

EXCERPT: GIRL BLUE

I was waiting, crouched behind his car in the parking lot. It was dark, and there were street lights but no cameras. I'd checked ahead of time. I'd planned this carefully, because I was going to kill him, no matter what. I figured I'd make it as easy as possible.

He came out of the bar, three sheets to the wind, which would make things so much easier. He listed to one side but tried real hard to stand up straight as he walked around the parking lot, awash in android-blue light, looking for his car. Then he took his key fob out and tapped it. The car beside me unlocked its doors and flashed its headlights. He saw it and smiled like he'd just won the lottery.

Only he hadn't won anything. His winning days were over.

He staggered to the car, opened the driver's door. I slipped up behind him, silent as a shadow, and jabbed him in the crease of his ass with a perfectly placed needle.

He spun around like a wobbling top, about to fall over. "What the hell!" he said and clocked me in the jaw. My head snapped sideways. I'd have gone down if I hadn't caught myself on the roof of his car. I stood ready to take another blow, thinking it would've been worse if he wasn't so drunk and wondering how long the drug would take to kick in.

He had one hand on his ass where I'd stuck him. His eyes rolled. I grabbed his shirt front, pulled him toward me as I opened the back door of his car. Then I turned him around, because I could not do this looking at him, and shoved him face-first onto the back seat. I climbed in after him, right up his back. He was out cold in seconds, not moving. I took the wood-handled garrote from my pocket. I'd made it out of picture-frame wire, several layers twisted together to make it thick, so I wouldn't accidentally decapitate him. I gagged a little as I put it over his head, and pulled it down between his face and the seat, over his chin to his neck. My inner voice, though it wasn't *really* mine, said, *Do it. Just do it. There's no other way. He won't feel anything. Just do it. You're so close.*

I pulled the right handle with my left hand, the left handle with my right, so they crossed at his nape. It was awful, what I was doing. My lips pulled back from my teeth with the effort it took—and not just physically. I had to *force* myself and my *self* was resisting. Tears filled my eyes. I tried to focus on my watch. It was an old-school watch, not a smart one. A delicate oval, with gold numbers and hands that swept way too slowly around its face. A narrow, pink leather band. After two minutes, he started to convulse, his body bucking underneath me, just like the internet said he would. I pulled tighter, to hold on, pressing my knees into his back like a cowboy at a rodeo. Terrible sounds started coming from him. Wet, growly, choky sounds. I wiped my wet face against my black, spandex-covered shoulder.

Just hold on. It's almost over. It's better this way. For everyone, even him.

I didn't know how many times the second hand had circled, but eventually it felt like it was over. The sounds stopped first, thank God. I'd never get them out of my head, though. Those sounds would haunt my dreams for the rest of my life. In silence, the twitching of his body eased, and he finally went still. I looked at my wristwatch and held the wood and wire weapon as tight as I could for three more minutes. My arm muscles were cramping up. My hands hurt despite the thick leather gloves I wore to protect them. Murder was not easy.

When I was sure he was dead, I let go of the garrote, slid it out from beneath him, and then climbed off him and backed down his body and out of the car. My legs were shaking so hard I wasn't sure I could stand up. But I did, I stood there beside the open car door, looking in at the man on the back seat.

I sniffed, backhanded my nose with my black leather glove, forced my gaze away from him to look around. A dozen vehicles, but no people. No witnesses. His keys were on the pavement, so I picked them up. His legs were still sticking out of the car. I bent them at the knees, so I could close the door.

Then I got behind the wheel and started the car, noticing for the first time that it was a Jaguar, a newish one. Blue or black, impossible to tell which in the dark.

I knew exactly where to put him. There was a burlap bag and a shovel already there, waiting.

I started the car. The radio blasted to life, scaring me so bad my head hit the ceiling before I got hold of myself and snapped the thing off. Then I sat there, gripping the wheel, white-knuckled. I took three long, deep breaths. Okay. I was okay. I put the car into gear and pulled out of the parking lot and onto the road.

I was driving through the night with a dead guy in the back seat, shaking all the way to my marrow. This was not me. This was not anything I'd ever imagined myself capable of, not in my wildest dreams.

Well, maybe in my *wildest* dreams.

A congested moan came from the back seat and sent a lightning bolt through my entire being.

197

The alarm clock went off like a freaking mind bomb.

The murderous dream popped like a balloon at a birthday party, showering its deadly latex bits all around me. I sat up fast, blurting an overly loud, "Holy fuck!"

Mason sprang out of bed, landing in a ready crouch beside it. "What? What?"

My bulldog picked up her head, blinked sightlessly at me, then lowered it and resumed snoring.

I looked around our bedroom like I was searching for an explanation. But there were only the soothing green walls and rich walnut trim.

"Rachel?" Mason turned on the lamp.

I couldn't look at him. Not yet. Lingering sparks of murder were still blinking out one by one in my head. I swallowed hard. "I'm okay. Bad dream."

"Was it?"

I met his eyes. "You know me too well."

"So? What was it?"

"I don't know yet."

Yes, you do. It's not like it's the first time a killer took up residence in your head, or you took up residence in his, after all.

It's not that, Inner Bitch.

Then what is it?

Like I just told Mason, I don't know yet.

Yes, you do.

"You okay?"

I slid up out of our big bed, planted a big, morning-breathy kiss on his face, and said, "I'd be better with coffee."

He smacked my butt and said, "Then coffee you shall have." He pulled on a pair of pajama bottoms and a T-shirt that said, DEFINITELY NOT A COP. Yes, I bought it for him. I think it's hilarious. He only wears it to humor me. What can I say? I've got myself a keeper.

I turned back toward the bed. "Wanna go outside, Myrt?"

Myrtle did not so much as twitch her ears in reply. "I guess not." I pulled on my fluffiest robe because it was six a.m. and also September, and went out onto the balcony. It had pretty wrought iron railings and a view of the four-mile-long, mile-wide Whitney Point Reservoir.

God, I loved *seeing*. I could spend hours just…seeing. As would, I guessed, anyone who'd spent twenty years of their life blind. I went to the railing and looked at the water. It was a rippled mirror, reflecting rolling hills and blue sky. The air tasted good, but its flavor was shifting. It smelled like back-to-school.

When Mason returned, he not only had our coffees, but a pair of blankets over his arm. He set the steaming mugs on the railing, and spread the blankets over our bowl-shaped wicker chairs in case there was dew on the cushions. I sank into mine, pulled the blanket around me, and he handed me my mug.

"You are the perfect man," I said. "I don't know if you know it or not, but–"

"I do know it." He dropped the second blanket on his chair, but didn't sit. He stood by the railing like I'd been doing. Only he wasn't looking, like I had been. He was thinking.

My man was a bit of a thinker. It was his greatest flaw.

"You miss Jeremy." It wasn't a question.

He glanced back at me. "I just don't *get* living on campus when campus is only thirty minutes away."

Three weeks ago, we'd moved Jeremy into his Binghamton University dorm. Mason seemed to think we'd moved him to the moon. "It's Labor Day weekend, Mace. He'll probably be back before breakfast and not leave again until Tuesday morning."

"Yeah." He still sounded mopey. "Think we'll see him this time, or he'll just drop off his laundry and go hang with his friends?"

"Wow. Clingy much?"

"Misty sees more of him than we do."

"You're an uncle. Misty is a girl, and she's better looking. Plus, she has her aunt's DNA, so I don't know how you can blame him. You know the females of the de Luca line are irresistible."

He sighed, staring out at the water. I stretched my leg to kick his backside. "That was funny. You didn't even crack a smile."

"Sorry. You're right. I know."

"Kids grow up. It happens. Get over it."

"Right. You were the one sniffling all the way home the day we moved him in."

"Freaking campus is a pollen pit. Sue me."

"You don't have allergies."

"Did that day."

I slid over in my chair, opened my blanket and patted the spot beside me. "BU is lots closer than the police academy, you know. You'd better toughen up by the time Jere heads to Albany." I was talking a good game, but I was missing Jeremy as much as Mason was. We might only be an uncle and an honorary aunt, but we'd been raising the boys for two years, and they felt like our own kids. Even though I wasn't nearly old enough for that.

Mason started to get in with me, then stopped because there was a ping from his PJ pocket. He pulled out his phone and looked at it.

"I reiterate my opinion," I said, "that this balcony should be a device-free zone."

"No such thing for a cop." He tapped the screen and said, "What's up, Rosie?"

Rosie was his partner. I hoped he was calling to invite us over for a barbecue.

At six-something a.m?

Yeah, probably not, I thought in reply to Inner Bitch's query. *I just hope it's not about what I dreamed.*

But it is. You know that, right?

I kind of did, but I didn't want to admit it. Not even to my subconscious Chatty Cathy.

Mason put the phone back into his pocket, and I'd missed

whatever else he'd said. But his face looked more serious than before. "I've gotta go. We have a body."

I closed my eyes. "A body?"

"Yeah. Joggers found him off the Rail Trial."

I could see the man from my dream in my mind's eye. A youthful fifty-something, fit, clean shaven, hair so light it was hard to spot the gray unless you were up close to it, with a yellow-orange tint like it had been red once. He had a perfectly bald spot the size of a silver dollar on the back of his head. I'd stared at that spot for an eternity last night.

A forefinger hooked under my chin. I opened my eyes to see my guy's worried ones trying to get a peek inside my head. He said, "Anything you need to tell me, Rachel?"

"Only if he drove a dark-colored Jag and was strangled. Or mostly strangled."

"Mostly strangled?"

"I woke up before he was all the way strangled. Might've had to bash his head in with a rock or something to get the job done, for all I know."

He swore softly, sinking onto the edge of my bowl chair, no easy feat. "You okay?"

"It was pretty vivid. He spun around and punched me in the jaw, and I swear it actually aches this morning." I tested my mouth-hinges experimentally, and sure as shit, the right one felt tender. "Then I was kneeling on his back, choking the life out of him with some kind of homemade garrote."

"Do you want to come along?" he asked.

"I don't want to leave Josh home alone."

"He's thirteen."

"Yeah, but I don't know what this is yet. So–"

"You saying it feels dangerous to you?"

"It feels...personal. Close." I rubbed my arms, set down my coffee and used his shoulders to pull myself up out of my comfy nest. "I need to shower. Like, now."

"So do I. Let me call in."

I went in to start without him.

The clay-tiled shower was double sized, with multiple heads. I adjusted the water, stepped in and let the hot spray blast the remnants of that dream away. There wasn't *always* a killer dragging me into mental ride-alongs, but it had been known to happen. The first time, it had been Mason's dead, serial-killer brother. Long story, but suffice it to say I got a little something extra from Eric Conroy Brown along with his donated corneal tissue. He opened some kind of door.

I knew things, felt things. I called it NFP for Not Fucking Psychic because I don't believe in psychics.

Mason stepped into the tiled shower. He moved into the spray beside me, turned around and scrubbed his hair. I watched him until he opened his eyes and looked back at me. And then he pushed my wet hair off my face, and tucked it behind my ear, and gave me that look that said everything I needed to hear. And I forgot what I'd been so upset about.

Mason was worried about Rachel. She'd been shaken by her dream. It had taken minutes for the fear to leave her eyes.

He parked where there was room, got out of his restored (by him) '74 Monte Carlo, and headed down Binghamton's popular walking trail. It ran alongside the Susquehanna River. Pleasant, usually. Not so much, now. Uniforms, forensics people, and his partner Rosie stood around a pile of freshly turned black earth, and a burlap shroud that wasn't quite big enough. A pale, dead arm stuck out from elbow to fingertips. Looked like the corpse was waving hello.

He walked closer. The murmur of the river drowned out the sounds of singing birds. The body was in a hole, sort of.

"Not even deep enough to cover the poor SOB," Rosie said. He had lost twenty pounds on his latest diet, which showed exactly nowhere. He was a big guy, his Rosie. They'd been partners since their rookie days. "Jogger spotted his hand, just sticking up outta the dirt. Can you imagine?"

"It'll make a great story, I guess."

"Yeah, eventually."

"Why the burlap? Why not just bury him?" Mason walked around the shallow grave to the bag's opening, picked up an edge with a pencil, and peered inside. "Flashlight?" he asked, hand out. Someone gave him one, cold steel cylinder in his palm, and he aimed it. "Ligature marks. Looks like he was strangled." *Or mostly strangled.* Something tickled up his spine. He shrugged it away.

"Anyone find an ID on him?" he asked.

"We're not patting him down for a wallet until we get him home where we can do it right." That was spoken with authority from a redhead with an ultra-short haircut. "Bag him up, burlap and all," she ordered. "Move him as little as possible. Don't shake off trace evidence."

As the team scrambled, she grinned at Mason. It was probably disrespectful to think she looked just like a Christmas elf. She had dimples, pink cheeks, intelligent green eyes, and a hairline that made her ears look ever so slightly pointed.

And she had her hand out, he finally noticed.

"Billie Carmichael. I'm the new forensic pathologist."

Thinking she looked about fourteen probably proved that he was getting old. "Mason Brown," he said.

"I know who you are, Detective Brown. I know your wife, too. I'm a huge fan."

"She's not my—"

"Careful!" The techs had dropped the body onto the gurney a little too hard, and the burlap came open.

Mason glimpsed the guy's face, either pudgy or starting to swell. His hair was mostly a pale orangey-gray. He looked back at the redhead. "What's an FP doing at a crime scene?"

"It's my first case. I couldn't wait." She said it with a grin, then forced a more serious expression.

"Since he's already bagged, you want to give me the rundown?" he asked. He was trying to remember ever being that happy to be at work, and failing.

"Male, mid-fifties, maybe a drinker. He was probably dumped last night," Billie Carmichael said. He liked her confident tone. "There's a car back by the trail head. Nobody else around. Might be his."

Rosie met Mason's eyes, brows raised, clearly impressed.

"What kind of car?" Mason asked.

"Jag," the new FP replied. "Nice one. Man I'd hate to die and leave a ride like that behind."

"Shit," Mason shook his head. "Shit."

His phone buzzed. It would be Rachel, asking about all this. He wished he didn't have to tell her, but knew he did. They didn't keep stuff from each other.

He walked a little bit away before looking at the text.

"Don't forget, BBQ at noon. Wayward nephew and all."

He got a good feeling from that message. He looked at Billie, and said, "You gonna be a while with the unboxing?"

"The unboxing. That's funny." Mason didn't smile, and she turned all business again. "I'm gonna work straight through the day on this guy."

"Good. I need to go home after I finish up here. Will you call me when I can come and get a look at the victim?"

"Yeah, sure."

Rosie said, "The Jag in the parking area is registered to Dwayne Clark. Got an address, phone number, and email. We're getting more info now."

"You got a phone number, you said?"

Rosie nodded, showing Mason his iPad.

"That's a cell number." Mason tapped it into the keypad of his phone, then silenced it and listened.

The guy in the burlap bag started ringing.

"Guess we've got a probable ID." He hung up the call. "Let's get some background on him."

"Already underway," Rosie said.

"Okay good." He looked at the ground around the makeshift grave. There were plenty of tracks in the dirt, thanks to the team that had dug the body out. "I hope you got a lot of shots of the ground before it was trampled," he said to the cop with the camera.

"I did." He brought his camera over and scrolled photos across its digital screen.

Mason looked at the images of the undisturbed grave. The killer had barely dug past the grass's knotted root carpet. He'd chopped it open, rolled it back, scraped out a little of the dirt underneath, and then tried to cover the unfortunate Dwayne Clark with it again.

Mason said, "Whoever put him here expected him to be found. Anything the body and this scene have to tell us could be significant. Let's not miss anything."

Billie's guys carried the dead man to an ambulance that had driven over the grass to get close. "The forensics team will finish up here," she said. "I want to stay with the body."

Mason said. "Listen, Carmichael, just so you know, we sometimes use Rachel as a consultant on cases like this."

"I know." Her elf-green eyes popped wider. "Are you bringing her in on *this one*? Wow, I didn't think I'd get to work with her so soon."

Oh, hell. "Listen, if you fangirl all over Rachel, she'll make you her slave. If you want her respect, treat her like an equal." It was a dumb request. Rachel had no equal, but still.

The change in Billie's expression was so sudden and deliberate he almost laughed. "I'll be completely professional, Detective. And I'll call you when I've finished with the exam." Then she unlocked her phone and handed it to him.

He entered his number into her contacts, then returned the phone. "Thanks."

He had to go home, host a family barbecue, and during a free moment break it to Rachel that her link to the darkness was back, big time.

Girl Blue

ALSO BY MAGGIE SHAYNE

The Fatal Series
Fatal Fixer Upper
Fatal, But Festive

The Secrets of Shadow Falls
Killing Me Softly
Kill Me Again
Kiss Me, Kill Me

The Shattered Sisters Series.
Reckless
Forgotten
Broken
Hollow
Hunted

Other Suspense Titles
The Gingerbread Man
Sleep with the Lights On
Wake to Darkness
Dream of Danger
Innocent Prey
Deadly Obsession
Cry Wolf
Girl Blue

ABOUT THE AUTHOR

New York Times bestselling author Maggie Shayne has published more than 50 novels and 23 novellas. She has written for 7 publishers and 2 soap operas, has racked up 15 Rita Award nominations and actually, finally, won the damn thing in 2005.

Maggie lives in a beautiful, century old, happily haunted farmhouse named "Serenity" in the wildest wilds of Cortland County, NY, with her soul-mate, Lance. They share a pair of English Mastiffs, Dozer & Daisy, and a little English Bulldog, Niblet, and the wise guardian and guru of them all, the feline Glory, who keeps the dogs firmly in their places. Maggie's a Wiccan high priestess (legal clergy even) and an avid follower of the Law of Attraction.

Find Maggie at http://maggieshayne.com

facebook.com/maggieshayneauthor
twitter.com#!/maggieshayne
instagram.com/maggieshayne
bookbub.com/authors/maggie-shayne

CPSIA information can be obtained
at www.ICGtesting.com
Printed in the USA
BVHW072135210423
662862BV00013B/543